3x (4/14) ✓ 11/14
9x 6/16 ✓ 4/17

Books by Carol Higgins Clark

Wrecked

Cursed

Zapped

Laced

Hitched

Burned

Popped

Jinxed

Fleeced

Twanged

Iced

Snagged

Decked

With Mary Higgins Clark

Dashing Through the Snow

Santa Cruise

The Christmas Thief

He Sees You When You're Sleeping

Deck the Halls

CAROL
HIGGINS CLARK

MOBBED

A Regan Reilly Mystery

SCRIBNER

New York   London   Toronto   Sydney

SCRIBNER
A Division of Simon & Schuster, Inc.
1230 Avenue of the Americas
New York, NY 10020

First Scribner hardcover edition April 2011

SCRIBNER and design are registered trademarks of The Gale Group, Inc.,
used under license by Simon & Schuster, Inc., the publisher of this work.

For information about special discounts for bulk purchases,
please contact Simon & Schuster Special Sales at
1-866-506-1949 or business@simonandschuster.com.

The Simon & Schuster Speakers Bureau can bring authors
to your live event. For more information or to book an event,
contact the Simon & Schuster Speakers Bureau at
1-866-248-3049 or visit our website at www.simonspeakers.com.

Designed by Carla Jayne Jones

Manufactured in the United States of America

1 3 5 7 9 10 8 6 4 2

Library of Congress Control Number: 2011924242
ISBN 978-1-4391-7028-1
ISBN 978-14391-7030-4 (ebook)

Acknowledgments

Kudos to the following people who helped get Regan Reilly to that garage sale!

As always, endless gratitude to my editor and friend Roz Lippel, for her guidance, support, and wonderful suggestions. Thanks Roz! Regan and Jack Reilly thank you as well!

Associate Director of Copyediting Gypsy da Silva.

Scribner Art Director Rex Bonomelli.

Senior Production Manager Lisa Erwin.

Copy Editor Joshua Cohen.

Scribner Publishing Associate Lisa Erickson.

Designer Carla Jayne Jones.

My agent, Esther Newberg.

My family and friends who cheer me on through the writing process.

A special thanks to my readers—I hope you enjoy Regan and Jack's unusual weekend at the shore!

In joyous memory of our uncle,
Kenneth John Clark
Known forever in our family as "The Unc"
1931–2011
You always made us laugh and always will
We love you

Kevin, Marilyn, Warren, Glenn, David, Carol, Brian, and Patty Clark
Billy and Tommy Quinn

MOBBED

Thursday, August 4th

1

G et that phone call over with." Jack Reilly leaned down, kissed his wife, then opened the front door of the loft they shared in TriBeCa.

"I will," Regan answered, with a slight grimace. "I had the feeling that guy wasn't going to turn out to be Mr. Right for Hayley, but I certainly didn't expect what we witnessed last night."

"He's a first-class creep," Jack said. "Hayley dodged a bullet."

"You're right," Regan agreed. "But somehow I don't think that will be the first thought that runs through her mind when I tell her what happened. It'll probably take a little time for her to reach that conclusion. Like another ten years."

Jack smiled, then started out the door. "If she has to hear the bad news from anyone, she's lucky it's you. You'll know what to say." He turned back and gave Regan a hug. "What a relief to be out of the singles scene. Another reason to raise a glass to your father."

Regan smiled. "That's for sure. And Dad never gets tired of hearing us thank him. We can toast him for the millionth time tonight."

Regan and Jack had met when Luke Reilly, owner of three funeral homes in New Jersey, had been kidnapped with his driver in New York City. He'd just stepped out of the hospital where Regan's mother, Nora, had been recovering from a broken leg. Jack, head of the Major Case Squad, had been called in. The rest, as they say, is history.

"Let's plan to be on the road by seven," Jack said as he stepped out into the hallway. "Hopefully the traffic will have eased up by then."

They were headed to the Jersey Shore to spend what was predicted to be a hot and sunny weekend with Regan's parents at the beach house they had purchased in Spring Lake, after spending years in the Hamptons. Saturday was Nora's birthday.

Regan smiled as she watched Jack turn and press the button for the elevator. He was the best thing that ever happened to her—and so handsome at six foot two with green eyes and light brown hair that tended to curl. Regan, five foot seven, was black Irish, with dark hair, blue eyes, and light skin. People often commented that they seemed made for each other.

The elevator door opened. "See you later, Regan Reilly Reilly," Jack said with a wave.

That was another thing. They had been born with the same last name. No messy paperwork for Regan when they got married.

"Love you," Regan called. She closed the door, then walked with deliberation to her office. A private investigator, she'd been living in Los Angeles at the time she met Jack and had a small, funky office in Hollywood. When she moved to New York, she'd set up shop in their spacious and painstakingly renovated loft. Heavy on the pain, Regan always said. The renovation had been no picnic. But it had been worth it.

The sight of her home office, with its gleaming mahogany desk and matching shelves filled with books and pictures, normally felt welcoming. But today was different. She wished she could have made this phone call last night, but Hayley had to work until well past midnight. Regan pulled out her chair, glancing at her grandmother's old-fashioned clock on the mantel as she sat down. It was 8:10. Hayley's cell phone number was on a piece of paper by the phone.

A high school classmate, Hayley Patton, had contacted Regan on Monday morning, just three days ago, after spending another miserable weekend without her beau. Scott Thompson, the guy she'd been dating for four months, had recently gone through a less than amicable divorce and claimed he needed to spend his weekends with his sixteen-year-old son, who lived with his mother.

"Until this all settles down, I have to focus on Trevor," he'd told her.

Scott lived and worked in northern New Jersey. Hayley was a rising star in the world of event planning and had a great apartment in New York City.

"Call me crazy," Hayley had said to Regan. "But how many sixteen-year-old boys want to spend nearly every Saturday night with Papa Bear?"

"Not many," Regan agreed.

Hayley's words came spilling out. "Scott can spend the day with the kid, then drive across the George Washington Bridge and have dinner with me. He's done it a few times, but I haven't seen him on a weekend in over a month. It's summertime. God forbid we should ever go to the beach like normal couples do. I'm going crazy. We have such a good time when we're together. He seems to really like me. And I like him. Maybe he does need time before getting involved in another relationship. But if he is giving me a line, I want to know *now*. He certainly loves going to the parties I bring him to—maybe a little too much." Hayley paused. "Regan, can I hire you to check him out?"

"Of course, Hayley," Regan had said. "When are you supposed to see him again?"

"Thursday."

"What's he doing the next few nights?"

"Beats me."

"I can start today by following him after work."

"Perfect!"

On Monday and Tuesday, Regan had tailed Scott after he left his office. Both nights he'd gone to the gym, then straight home. Yesterday, after putting in late hours the two nights before, Jack left work early and accompanied Regan on her surveillance.

Regan reached for the phone. Here goes nothing, she thought, as she dialed Hayley's number.

"Regan!" Hayley cried, answering on the first ring. It sounded as if she were out on the street—horns were blowing and a siren was wailing in the distance. "Scott just texted me he has to cancel our date tonight. He said he'd call later. Do you have any news?"

"Yes, I do."

"I can tell by your tone it's not good."

Regan frowned. "No, it isn't."

Hayley groaned. "He really wanted to come to the premiere with me last night, but I couldn't bring anyone. There was such tight security with all those stars. He even called me yesterday, hinting around for an invitation. Where did he end up?"

Oh boy, Regan thought. Here goes. "Hayley, he was out with someone who—"

"I knew he must be dating someone else!" Hayley interrupted. "Did they look like they were having a good time?"

"Well," Regan said, then paused. "Hayley, I might as well just say it. Scott got engaged last night."

"*Engaged?!*"

"Yes. Jack was with me. We followed Scott from his office to a restaurant an hour south. After he'd gone inside, we waited for about fifteen minutes, then went in and sat at a table near his. He was with a woman . . ."

"Did you hear him propose?" Hayley practically shrieked.

"Not exactly. It was a Chinese restaurant. When she cracked open her fortune cookie, the ring fell out."

"So what happened then?"

"I gues the fortune said, 'Will you marry me?' She screamed, said yes, and the waiters started clapping."

"How embarrassing!"

"You're right," Regan agreed. "This was *not* the guy for you."

"Was she pretty?"

"Well," Regan began.

"I don't want to hear it," Hayley interrupted. Her voice cracked. "He must have been planning this for a while. Why did he string me along? Just to be able to go to A-list parties and hot nightclubs? Was he just waiting to see if he'd get to go to the premiere last night before he dumped me?"

"I don't know, Hayley. But you're better off without him. He must have been lying to this other woman, too."

"Regan, I'm going to get back at him. Somehow. I'll figure it out. He'll be sorry, believe me."

"Hayley, be careful. Forget him. You'll meet someone else. You're out all the time . . ."

"That's what everyone says, but it's not easy. I work hard at these events. It's business. Last year I tried an Internet dating service, and what happened? They set me up with my brother!"

"I know," Regan said sympathetically.

"I have to run to the subway. I'll call you later, okay?" Hayley asked quickly, sounding as if she were trying not to cry.

"Call me anytime, Hayley. You have my cell number."

"Thanks. 'Bye"

That guy is really a jerk, Regan thought as she hung up the phone and headed into the kitchen. If he had gone to the premiere with Hayley, when would he have proposed to that girl? Tonight?

The phone rang as Regan was pouring herself a cup of coffee. She reached for the receiver on the wall.

"Hello."

"Regan, I'm going to get back at him!" Hayley shouted vehemently. Regan could hear the roar of the subway in the background. "I don't know how, but I'll figure something out. Talk to you later."

The phone clicked in Regan's ear. A moment later it rang again. She's so upset, Regan thought as she answered, expecting to hear more specific plans for Hayley's revenge.

But it was her mother.

"Hi, Mom. I thought you'd be writing now."

Nora Regan Reilly was a well-known suspense writer who liked to hit the computer by six A.M.

"I was," Nora said, "but, Regan, can you do me a favor and take the train down this morning?"

"Sure. What's up?"

"I just received a frantic phone call from Karen Fulton. She's the high school friend I reconnected with at our reunion in the spring, who lives in San Diego. She just got word that her mother, the irrepressible Edna Frawley, sold their house here at the shore in Bay Head."

"Didn't you stay at that house way back when?" Regan asked.

"Way back when?" Nora repeated with a chuckle. "Thanks, Regan. The answer is yes."

"I didn't mean it was *that* long ago," Regan protested.

"Anyway," Nora continued, "Edna is having a big garage sale

today. She rented a plane to fly over the beach touting the sale and has a full-page ad in the local paper. Everything the actress Cleo Paradise left behind when she rented the house last month is up for grabs. Karen's afraid everything from her childhood will be gone. She's getting on a plane but won't be in until tonight. She asked me to go over there and see what's going on. I'd love for you to come with me."

"I'll check the train schedule," Regan said as she walked back into her office. "Karen's mother sounds like a character."

"She is. I remember her well. With Edna Frawley you can always expect the unexpected."

Like Scott, Regan thought, picturing in her mind the scene at the Chinese restaurant. His proposal to that girl certainly was unexpected. And now Hayley was intent on revenge.

Regan suddenly felt anxious. If Hayley crosses him, who knows what else "unexpected" he's capable of?

2

Twenty-seven minutes earlier

I can't believe my ears!" Karen Fulton wailed.

Edna Frawley held the phone at arm's length, her daughter's noisy hysteria a jarring contrast to the peaceful stillness of the morning air. My little baby sounds as if she's right here by my side instead of three thousand miles away in California, Edna mused as she patted her coiffed strawberry blond hair. Seventy-eight-year-old Edna was ready for action. Fully made up, dressed in a jumpsuit she'd worn in the sixties, she was relaxing in her backyard gazebo, counting the minutes until the arrival of her garage sale guests. Hopefully a camera crew or two as well.

"It's time, darling," Edna said cheerily as she reached for her coffee. "When opportunity knocks, I answer."

"But you answered the door to a total stranger!"

"The total stranger rang the bell at the gate. The total stranger wants to pay me a respectable sum for this house. At a time when no one is buying."

"But you weren't selling!"

"Which is even more perfect because I don't have to pay a Realtor's commission."

"But that's our shore house," Karen protested. "It's where I spent my summers since childhood. It's where you retired . . . all those priceless memories."

"You were always complaining we were in too ritzy a section. Not close enough to the boardwalk with the bumper cars, not close enough to—"

"I know, but I was a kid," Karen interrupted. "We were lucky to have such a beautiful house like that, even though it's not right on the beach."

"Your father was obsessed with erosion. If we lived on the water, he'd have been out there with a ruler every day." Edna sighed. "Don't get me wrong, darling. I'll be sorry to say good-bye to the lovely backyard, the pool, the sense of privacy. This place has charm. But with today's market, I could be dead and buried before we'd get a buyer who would fork over the priceless sum you think your memories are worth."

"I wish you had talked to me about it first."

"What's to talk about? And how often do you visit? Once or twice a year? Ever since your father passed over, six long years ago, I've been rumbling around this house by myself. Arnetta was always telling me I should rent my house for at least a month during the summer, make some cash, and stay with her in the retirement village to see how I liked it. I could kiss her feet. Staying with Arnetta at Golden Peaks was a blast. Now I can buy a place there!"

"I thought Arnetta got on your nerves."

"She's grown on me."

"But why can't you take a little time with this? We'll go through everything in the house together, then you can have the sale."

"The train's already left the station, sweetie. Besides, this gentleman wants to move in as soon as possible. And I'm so lucky to have the things Cleo Paradise left behind to put on sale. People will show up who would never have dreamt of coming by. Hopefully I'll get rid of every last bit of junk in our attic and basement. It's been quite an adventure sorting through everything."

"Don't sell my things!"

"They're in quarantine."

"Mom, I don't think you have the right to sell whatever Cleo Paradise left behind. Don't you have to notify her and give her a certain amount of time to come back and retrieve her possessions?"

"Another lucky break! She left a letter that I found when I came back here on Sunday. I was hoping to see her but she left a few days early. She apologized for anything out of order, told me to keep the security deposit, and do what I wanted with whatever she forgot. I have it in black and white. She was a little bit of a slob so I call it even steven."

"Well, you shouldn't have put her name in the ad."

"Why not?"

"It doesn't seem right. I thought you liked her."

"She was a sweet girl, even though she refused my invitation to take her to the club for lunch. You know what touched my heart about her?"

"What?" Karen asked flatly.

"She said she couldn't wait to curl up in the gazebo and read a book. Your father and I sat here so many summer nights . . ." Edna's voice trailed off.

"It's where I had my first kiss," Karen recalled.

"Don't remind me," Edna retorted. "I never liked that kid. What was his crazy nickname?"

"Fish."

"Oh, that's right. He liked to swim. His fingers were always wrinkled." Edna rolled her eyes. "Karen, this is all good news.

When I came back Sunday I was feeling a little down in the dumps. On the one hand it was good to come home, and on the other I hated leaving my new friends at Golden Peaks. I was making a cup of tea, which my grandmother said she always did to feel better if the blues hit her before cocktail hour. I was just about to take my first sip when the doorbell rang. It was fate! Later that night, kooks were driving by, honking their horns, shouting Cleo's name. I was so glad I'd agreed to sell the house. Even though we have the gate and the alarm system, I don't feel safe here anymore . . ." Edna paused for a moment to allow that tidbit to sink into her daughter's brain. "At Golden Peaks, I won't be so completely alone."

"You know I wish I could live closer to you. But Hank's company is headquartered in San Diego."

"He does research on the algae in the Pacific Ocean. What's wrong with the algae in the Atlantic?" Edna asked for the umpteenth time. "The Atlantic's right down the block. If you lived with me, he could walk to work."

Karen sighed. "Does Frankie know about any of this?"

"Highly doubtful. What ocean is he in the middle of as we speak? Tinkling the ivories on a cruise ship keeps my son busy. He won't care. He's never here, either. I wish I had raised at least one homebody."

"Do you have anyone helping you run the sale?"

"Two lovely young women who have a business called The Garage Sale Gurus. I was lucky to find them."

"What about security?"

"Two young, handsome, muscular men. Oh, to be a girl again . . ."

"Who are they?"

"Bouncers at one of the clubs in Asbury Park. They come highly recommended. Tattoos and all." Edna stood and surveyed the backyard. The pool was sparkling in the sunlight. The tall hedges that bordered the wrought iron fence were green and lush. And every inch of the lawn was covered with junk. "I'm starting a new life, sweetie. It's so exciting. I feel young again. And with my aches and pains, that's not easy."

"I'm calling the airlines."

"It will be wonderful to see you. And when I do there's another big surprise I'll tell you about."

"What?" Karen asked hastily.

"It wouldn't be a surprise if I told you, now, would it?" Edna asked, then gleefully hung up the phone.

3

After Regan checked the train schedule, she hurried into the bedroom. A train was leaving Penn Station in an hour. I'm glad that for once I started packing in advance, she thought as she tossed more clothes into her suitcase.

Regan couldn't stop thinking about Hayley and how upset she was. I wish there was some great guy I could introduce her to, Regan thought as she gathered her toiletries. But if there were, Kit would kill me if I didn't introduce her first.

Kit was Regan's best friend, who lived in Hartford and worked for an insurance company. They'd met in junior year of college when they'd spent a semester in England. Kit was still searching for Mr. Right. Since Regan found Jack, she was always on the lookout for someone for Kit.

So far, the pickings had been slim. Kit had spent the Fourth of July weekend with them in Spring Lake. Regan set Kit up on a blind date that had been a disaster. Thinking back on the moment Kit came back to the house after dinner, Regan laughed out loud.

"Regan!" Kit had cried. "Are you out of your mind?"

"Was it that bad?" Regan asked meekly.

"That bad? It was worse. When you told me that you and Jack

met him on the beach, I had such a fantasy in my mind of what he'd be like," Kit said with amazement. "Okay, he's my age, single, not bad looking and well educated, but I never imagined he'd spend the entire evening discussing his fascination with invertebrates."

"Invertebrates?"

"Invertebrates."

"When I got stung by a jellyfish he was very helpful," Regan explained. "He had vinegar in his bag that he put on my leg. He knew exactly what to do."

"Didn't that give you a hint of what he was like?" Kit had asked incredulously. "Most of the guys I dated never bring suntan lotion to the beach. This guy had a supply of vinegar! And listen to this: when we sat down he gave me one of those wipes for your hands. And he asked for separate bread baskets."

"He does sound strange. But I'm trying, Kit."

"And please don't stop." Kit paused for a millisecond. "I appreciate your efforts on my behalf, Regan. I really do. But this guy was *obsessed* by creatures without spinal columns."

"Then there's no way you'd be right for each other," Regan laughed.

Glancing at the clock radio, Regan started to move faster. She closed her suitcase, reached for the phone, and dialed Jack's number.

"Everything okay?" he asked quickly.

"Yes, fine," Regan said. "My mother called," she began, then quickly filled him in on the garage sale.

"How did Cleo Paradise end up renting the house?"

"I don't know. To think that last year at this time she was a virtual unknown. Then she had a hit movie and was nominated for an Academy Award. Now her name is being exploited to get people to come to a garage sale."

"I think Cleo Paradise probably likes being famous, but it has its price. She didn't win the Academy Award, her next movie bombed, which thrilled a lot of people, now she's starring in a garage sale. The question is, why would she have left so much stuff behind?"

"Who knows? Maybe there's not much there."

"By the way, did you reach Hayley?"

"Yes. Needless to say, she's very upset. She's also bent on revenge, which worries me. I hope she calms down. Jack, I've got to run. My bag is packed. If you don't mind bringing it with you tonight . . ."

"Of course. Regan, be careful."

Regan smiled. It was what Jack said to her all the time. And she never tired of hearing it. "I will."

Outside, even though it was still early, the sun was blazing. Regan flagged down a cab. She got in, shut the door, and said, "Penn Station, please."

Without a word, the driver accelerated. I guess he heard me, Regan thought as the cab lurched forward. Then she heard the mumbling. Another driver illegally chatting on his cell phone. What do these guys talk about for hours on end?

At Penn Station, Regan paid, giving a good tip for which her driver showed not an ounce of gratitude. But if I didn't give him a decent tip, Regan thought as she put her wallet back in her purse, I'd feel guilty. No winning in this situation. She got out, hurried across the sidewalk to the escalator, and as it descended could see that there were already plenty of travelers, many dressed in shorts and T-shirts, wheeling their suitcases around the station. It was August and the forecast was for a sunny, hot, beautiful weekend.

Regan bought a ticket and a cup of coffee. Moments later she was settling in on the train. She got out her computer, sent a quick e-mail to Hayley telling her to hang in there and that she'd call her later, then did a search on Cleo Paradise. Several photos of the petite actress popped up. She had light brown hair, porcelain skin, and beautiful green eyes.

Cleo was an only child whose parents had changed their last name to Paradise after they were married and started Paradise Adventures, a travel company that led explorers on expeditions all over the globe. For twenty-five years they roamed the planet before Cleo was born. Having a baby didn't stop them. Cleo in tow, they never stopped moving. You name it, they've been there, done that. The Arctic, the Amazon, the North Pole, the Brazilian rainforest. They trekked the Himalayas, slept in caves, camped in the desert with Bedouins, and enjoyed the thrill of shipwreck diving surrounded by sharks. Cleo's parents no longer had the company but they were still on the go. Everywhere they went they collected artifacts. They planned to open a museum when they finally decided they were too old to travel. If ever!

Regan shook her head. With this background, how on earth did Cleo end up at Edna Frawley's home in a quiet little town in New Jersey?

But then again, Regan thought after a moment, maybe it's not so surprising. Maybe she wanted to be still and enjoy a little peace out of the spotlight.

Instead she got a landlord like Edna Frawley.

———————◆———————

4

Cleo's eyes widened as she read from her computer screen. "She's selling my things at a garage sale! It must be the clothes I left in the washer and dryer. That miserable woman!" she blurted. "I wished I'd never rented her house! I should have known she was trouble the minute I met her."

Cleo was seated at a little log desk in her rental cabin, in the only log cabin camp in the state of New Jersey, seventy miles west of Camp Edna. The resort had been created by thirty-two-year-old Dirk Tapper, a man who loved the experience of frontier living and didn't think people in his home state of New Jersey should have to travel halfway across the country to find it. Growing up, his favorite television show was reruns of *Bonanza*. As a child Tapper longed to have a horse and a corral and a barn. He never tired of watching Little Joe and Hoss and Adam and Pa jump on their horses and gallop toward adventure. He wanted to live like that, but it wasn't meant to be. He grew up in a two-family home in Central Jersey, his grandparents in the upstairs unit. To satisfy his cowboy craving, his father took him to a dude ranch when he was seven. Little Dirk Tapper was hooked.

After high school he went to college out West and worked on

a ranch but was too homesick to stay. His was a tight-knit clan, just like the Cartwrights. The lonesome cowboy came back after graduation, got a landscaping job, saved up for years, found some investors, then bought a large piece of wooded property with a huge lake and built a log cabin resort, promising a serene experience in a rustic setting.

Tapper's advertisement for his venture pointed out that the first log cabin in this country had been built in Swedesboro, New Jersey, and although the Jersey Shore was wonderful, the woods were great, too. "You can swing from a hammock nestled in the trees, sunbathe on the lake, ride horses on our trails. Go back in time and live the good life. Forget the modern world."

Cleo had found the camp online. When she drove away from Edna's, she was looking for another place to hide.

After what she'd gone through the last several months, she wanted to get away from Hollywood. The Hamptons was Hollywood East, so she looked for a place at the Jersey Shore. The original plan was for Cleo and her best friend, Daisy, to drive cross-country together and spend the month at Edna's. They'd relax at the pool, walk the beach, go into New York City to see shows. Then Daisy, a struggling actress who never begrudged Cleo her success, was cast in a movie. So Cleo went alone. She packed up her SUV and drove from Los Angeles to New Jersey. She checked into motels along the way using credit cards she'd taken out under the name Connie Long, so no one would bother her. It was a grueling, lonely trip. Finally, she reached Edna's. Edna came running out of the house and greeted her with outstretched arms. Lonesome as Cleo felt, there was no way she was going to get friendly with the woman who she could tell right away was a busybody.

Cleo swam and relaxed and read but had no company. She spoke to Daisy on the phone every few days and received occasional e-mails from her parents who were in a far-flung area of eastern Europe. But she was itching for company. She ventured into town and made the mistake of letting her guard down. She chatted with people at the coffee shop and the pub and at the supermarket. It wasn't long before she came home at night to find a dozen roses with wilted petals and thorny stems thrown inside the gate.

Just like she'd found on her car in Los Angeles.

She was terrified.

But she felt foolish calling the police. In her movie that bombed, she was the victim of a deranged stalker, someone who left her dead roses. If she reported the incident, the press would have a field day. They might think she was making it up to get attention. But it had happened before. Was it the same person who had left the flowers in Los Angeles? Or someone else who had seen that embarrassing movie and came up with the same sick idea?

Cleo tried to ignore it when it happened again a week later. But the third time she found dead flowers at Edna's, they were by the front door, and there was a note covered with bloodstains. Cleo packed up her car and fled. She didn't want to tell Daisy and worry her. Daisy was in the Florida Everglades, covered with insect bites, finishing her movie. As soon as the movie wrapped, hopefully soon, she'd fly to Newark. Cleo would pick her up and they'd drive back to California together. The log cabin resort seemed like the perfect place to disappear and wait for Daisy.

As Cleo sat at her computer, she remembered how scared she'd been when she read the note.

CLEO GET OUT OF HERE BEFORE YOU GET HURT.

It's a miracle I was able to make myself go back in the house and pack anything, she thought. Cleo put her head down on the log cabin desk. She felt a splinter in her forehead and bolted back up.

That note I left! I said I was leaving early to do a role in a big movie. I needed an excuse because I told Edna I'd be there when she got back on Sunday. Is she blabbing to everyone about that?

A knock at the door startled her. She called out, "Can I help you?"

"Miss Long?"

"Yes."

"It's Gordy from the front desk. The boss doesn't think I properly welcomed the people who checked in this morning. So I'm trying to go out of my way for everybody. I'm going down to the market. I was wondering if you needed anything. You've been in there by yourself for several days now . . ."

Cleo rolled her eyes. She'd told them she was writing a book on meditation but was sure that Dirk Tapper didn't buy it, even though she didn't think he recognized her. He had appeared at the door the other night asking if she wanted to roast marshmallows at the campfire with the rest of the gang. She'd declined the offer. Now she'd decline Gordy's.

"Thank you, Gordy, but I'm fine."

"Are you sure?"

"Yes. I'd open the door but I'm still in my bathrobe."

"You sound like my mom. She doesn't like to be seen with curlers in her hair."

Cleo grimaced. What's happening to my life? she wondered. She pretended to laugh. "Thanks anyway."

"Okay. If you need anything at all, just call the front desk."

"I will." Cleo waited, then peered out the curtain. The tall, gangly boy was heading down the wooded trail, his arms swinging. He means well, Cleo thought. But isn't this place supposed to offer privacy?

Cleo went back to her computer to see if there was anything else online about the garage sale. In the comments section below the story, someone had just written, *"I hear you're off doing another movie, Cleo. No dead flowers in this one, I hope!"*

5

Cliff and Yaya Paradise were heading back to their campsite in Ukraine, often incorrectly referred to as "the" Ukraine. They were staying in a campground in the mountains, close to the Black Sea, and the ruins of enough ancient castles to keep the most die-hard tourist busy. They'd been at an all-day dance class down in the valley. Naturally they had dressed for the part, wearing the traditional garb of the Ukrainian folk dancers. Cliff was an attractive man with gray hair and a robust build. His petite wife had white-blond hair and delicate features.

"Yaya, I'm tired," Cliff said. "I never thought I'd say it, but I am."

"That dancing was strenuous," Yaya answered. "That instructor really swung you around the room. I think she had a crush on you."

"You're making me blush, my sweet."

"You've never blushed in your life."

"True enough! Yaya, think of how impressed everyone will be when we perform the dances of so many different cultures at our joint seventieth birthday party."

"Darling, who are we going to invite? We don't have many friends left. We're off everyone's holiday card list."

Cliff waved his hand. "That's because no one knows where we are. But if we have a party, everyone will be there, I can assure you of that. Let's have it in New York over the holidays. We should start planning."

Yaya reached for Cliff's hand as they trudged up the mountain. "We should also think about spending more time in California. I miss Cleo terribly."

"She could have come with us on this trip," Cliff said. "But she said no."

"The poor dear wanted to relax. She's had so much this year. Ups and downs and ups and downs. I do wish she'd get a role she could sink her teeth into after she gets rid of that ghastly agent. And I wish she'd let us take her to a spiritual retreat in Tibet. We'd have a wonderful time."

"She's finding her way in the world, my dear," Cliff said. "She's independent and headstrong. But you're right. I miss her, too." He turned to his wife of forty-nine years. "A strange feeling just came over me."

"What kind of feeling?"

"We should head to New Jersey."

"What?"

"We've never been there."

"No, we haven't."

"We've been all over the world but never to New Jersey. Cleo is still there, isn't she?"

"Yes. The woman whose house she's renting said she could extend her stay if she'd like. I think that's what Cleo was planning to do. She was waiting for Daisy to finish her movie in the Everglades."

"We've never been there, either."

"No, we haven't. Cleo said the Jersey Shore is beautiful."

"Jersey Shore? I've never heard of it."

"It's the term for the beach towns along the coastline in New Jersey. It extends for more than one hundred miles. I'll have you know that people in New Jersey refer to it simply as 'the Shore.'"

"It sounds lovely. Let's head back to the States, visit our daughter at 'the Shore,' plan our birthday party, and start scouting locations for our museum. Perhaps New Jersey would be a good setting. By now our trunk of treasures should have arrived at the house where Cleo is staying, shouldn't it?"

"Oh yes. I received a delivery confirmation when I checked our e-mail last week."

"Marvelous. Tomorrow we'll head down into the valley where we can log onto the Internet and e-mail Cleo. We'll tell her we're on our way. I can't wait to go through that big trunk and show Cleo each and every artifact we've lovingly collected on this trip. Treasures we want to share with the world."

"Cliff," Yaya said breathlessly. "I'm so lucky to have you."

He patted her arm and raised an eyebrow. "I know."

They burst into laughter and together continued up the mountain.

"Cleo will be so excited," Yaya said. "I just know she will."

"Absolutely. She didn't expect to see us again for months."

6

I am not going to let Cleo Paradise get away with it.

She can run, but she can't hide. I can't wait to make her regret what she's done.

Never again will she worry about bad scripts.

Or dead flowers.

7

Regan had been staring out the window when the conductor's voice came over the announcement system. "Next stop, Spring Lake. Please look around your seat and make sure you have all your belongings . . ."

Regan put her laptop computer back in its case. As the train slowly rolled into the station, she got up and walked toward the exit. When she stepped outside, the air felt even hotter than before.

"Regan! I'm over here!" Nora called.

Regan turned her head. Nora, wearing oversized sunglasses, chic summer pants, blouse, and sandals, was standing by her Mercedes, waving her arms.

Smiling, Regan hurried over.

"Hi, darling, how was your trip?" Nora asked as she and Regan hugged.

"Fine." Regan opened the back door, placed her bag on the floor, then got into the driver's seat as Nora went around to the passenger side. Ever since Regan got her driver's license, she'd always been the driver when she was with Nora. Nora was happy to relinquish the wheel. Regan and Luke always joked that driving with Nora made them seasick. She didn't keep her foot steady on the gas, preferring to apply pressure only when she felt the car slowing down. Which was every three seconds.

"I programmed the address into the navigation system," Nora said as the two of them fastened their seat belts. "It should take us no time to get there."

"Does this woman have any idea you're coming?" Regan asked.

"No."

"What time does the sale start?"

"Noon. Regan, I didn't ask you on the phone. Anything happen last night with the guy Hayley is dating?"

Regan put the car into drive and steered out of the parking lot. "*Was* dating."

"Was dating? What happened?"

"He got engaged . . ."

Nora shook her head as Regan recounted the tale of Scott's fortune cookie proposal. "What is it with these guys?" she asked.

"I don't know."

"What did this bird do for a living?"

"Something in finance," Regan said. "Poor Hayley. I hadn't talked to her in so long. I was sorry it had to be under those circumstances." She paused for a moment. "When is the last time you saw this Edna Frawley?"

"High school."

"Really?"

"Yes. Way back when."

Regan smiled. "I'm never going to live that down."

They drove toward Bay Head. It was a gorgeous day.

Twenty minutes later they reached the treelined street that the navigation device called their "final destination."

"This is nice," Regan said.

"It's always been a lovely area," Nora agreed. "I remember

once when I stayed with Karen, Edna offered to take us to the movies. When Karen was in line for popcorn, Edna asked me for the money for my ticket."

"You're kidding."

Nora laughed. "I'm not."

"I can't wait to meet her," Regan said.

"It sounds like she hasn't changed much," Nora commented. "Look at that line of people!"

As the house came into view, so did the throngs of people waiting outside the gate.

"There's no place to park," Regan said. "Do you want me to drop you off and I'll find a space?"

"No. Look, Regan, there's someone pulling out down the block. Let's grab that spot."

It took Regan three attempts to parallel park the car.

Nora smiled. "I can't keep my foot on the gas, you can't parallel park."

They got out and hurried back to the gate, where a ponytailed young woman was handing out tickets. Regan almost stopped dead in her tracks.

It was Scott's fiancé.

8

All morning Hayley sat in her office overlooking the Hudson River, fielding congratulatory calls about the wonderful party she'd organized last night. Framed movie posters hung on the brick walls, movies whose premiere parties Hayley had also planned.

"It was too fabulous, darling. And you looked gorgeous. So stylish."

"Hayley, you outdid yourself. Everything ran smooth as silk!"

"Those pigs in a blanket were divine! I love that you had the nerve to serve them!"

Reeling from the news about Scott's engagement, Hayley did her best to pretend she was on cloud nine. She was too embarrassed to say a word about Regan's shocking find to her twenty-three-year-old assistant. Angie had a terrific boyfriend she'd been dating since college. I hope they get married soon, Hayley thought. Dating is torture.

Hayley had just hung up the phone when Angie knocked on the door.

"Hayley?"

Hayley looked up. "Yes, come in."

Angie appeared in the doorway. Small and blond, she had

a pretty face and a sweet smile. But she could be tough when Hayley needed her to be. Like keeping gate-crashers out of parties who tried to pretend they were on the guest list.

"I wanted to remind you about your lunch date. It's getting a little late."

"Thanks, Angie. Of course. I'm a little tired and with everyone calling . . ."

Angie nodded. "You did a great job last night. I have so many e-mails from potential clients to go over with you when you get back. Everyone wants you to plan their events. You're hot!"

Not that hot, Hayley thought. But she smiled. "The trick is to keep it going. In this business, there's always someone new coming down the pike who wants to copy your style, grab your connections . . ."

"There's no one like you, Hayley," Angie said, perhaps a little too brightly.

Hayley got up, went into the little bathroom off her office, and looked in the mirror. I look so drained, she thought. I definitely need more makeup. She brushed her long, highlighted hair and applied blush and lipstick. One thing about being an event planner, she thought, is that you always have to be upbeat and look alive. People don't want sad sacks to plan their parties. Hayley had a lunch date with a producer whose Broadway play would be opening in October. Word was the script wasn't great, but this woman was determined to have a blowout when the curtain went down.

Hayley put her makeup back in her cosmetics bag, zipped her purse, and headed to the outer office.

"I'll be back in a few hours," she said to Angie. "Hold down the fort."

"I will. Have fun!"

Hayley walked into the hallway and pressed the button for

the elevator. The building had been a warehouse before it was converted to offices. It was a hip place to work, brimming with the energy of numerous twentysomethings, excited about their careers, anxious to grab every opportunity New York City had to offer. The elevator door finally opened. Hayley stepped inside. As the door closed her cell phone rang. She looked at the caller ID. It was Scott! If Hayley didn't feel alive before, she did now. So alive she felt as if she'd just stuck her finger in a socket.

A couple other people were on the elevator, no one Hayley recognized. For a moment she debated whether to answer. Finally she couldn't help herself.

"Hello," she said quickly. "I'm on an elevator . . ."

"Hey," Scott said, his voice dripping with affection. "How did it go last night?"

"Great," Hayley answered curtly. "How was your night?"

"I took my son to the movies."

"How nice."

"It is. It's especially nice because I saw him last night instead of Saturday. One of his friends is having a party. Which means I'm free to go out with you. What do you say, Hayley? I want to make it a perfect evening."

The elevator door opened at the ground floor. Hayley stepped into the lobby. The expression on her face would have stopped a clock.

"Hayley?" Scott asked. "Are you there?"

"I'm here," Hayley said. "I'd love to see you Saturday night, Scott. It will be nothing less than perfect."

"I can't wait."

You say that now, Hayley thought, grinning wickedly. But our date will be one of my most carefully planned events ever. And one of my biggest. One that you'll wish you never attended.

9

Inside her home, Edna had just started chatting with Mark Peabody, a young reporter from a paper she had never heard of. They were standing in the spacious vestibule. Peabody had a camera and was streaming their interview live on the Internet.

"As you can see," Edna said, pointing to the wall where the letter Cleo had written her was hanging in a frame, "Cleo left me to do as I saw fit with her things."

"Fascinating," the earnest young man said as he trained the camera on the letter. "Just fascinating. She says she was offered a role in an exciting new movie. I hope it's better than her last one. Did you see *You Don't Bring Me Flowers, Alive or Dead*?"

"Yes."

"Don't you think that was a terrible career choice?"

"How am I supposed to know? I'm not her agent. And she's off doing another movie so it hasn't stopped her."

"Good point. It's just that the role in *My Super Super* was so perfectly suited to the talent and charisma of Cleo Paradise. So perfect she received an Academy Award nomination. I watch that movie over and over. Cleo was hilarious as the nutty super-intendent."

And she wouldn't let me take her to lunch, Edna thought. I

could have used a few laughs. "It sounds like you have a crush on her."

"Oh . . . ," Mark said. "What guy wouldn't?" Nervously he cleared his throat. "Can we get a look at what you're selling of Cleo's? I'm sure that folks all over the world who can't make it to the sale would love a peek . . ."

"Folks all over the world?" Edna asked.

"Of course. The Internet is the World Wide Web."

"That doesn't mean everyone's watching."

"You never know, Mrs. Frawley."

"I should have had operators standing by," Edna muttered. "Follow me." She led him into the dining room and pointed at the table.

"Wow!" Peabody cried. "Maybe Cleo does prefer the dark side of life. I'm sure a lot of people will want to get a look at this!"

The dining room table was covered with skulls.

10

Edna's offspring was a nervous wreck. It's a good thing I woke up so early this morning, Karen thought as she raced to the gate at San Diego International Airport, where her flight to Newark was already boarding. If I hadn't had such trouble sleeping last night, I still might not have looked at that e-mail. I'd have slept until eight, pulled on my gym clothes, and gone to a Pilates class. Then I'd have come home and relaxed and read the paper. Then maybe I would have checked my e-mail.

Karen had dragged herself out of bed at 4:30. She'd heard that if you couldn't sleep, you should get up and do something to get your mind off the fact you had insomnia. For hours she'd tossed and turned, trying to decide whether to follow that advice.

Finally she decided to listen to the experts. She dragged herself out of bed, went into the kitchen, turned on her computer, and read the e-mail from her childhood friend who had seen the ad for the garage sale.

"Your house is sold!" Donna Crumby had written. She had a bakery near where they grew up and was the world's leading gossip. "I'm so sorry! We had so much fun at your pool parties. Remember those three-legged races?"

Karen was blown away. "No wonder I couldn't sleep!" she'd growled, slamming her computer mouse down on the counter. "I knew something was brewing. I swear I'm psychic when it comes to my mother!"

A seventh-grade teacher, Karen also taught summer school. The session had ended last week. Since then she'd been relishing her free time. Not anymore.

After calling her mother, then the airlines, then Nora Regan Reilly, Karen had gone back into the bedroom. Hank woke up when she pulled her suitcase off the shelf in the closet and it came crashing to the floor.

"My mother sold the house without telling me!" Karen shrieked. "The woman talks my ear off about every little thing. What she had for breakfast, lunch, dinner, every boring detail of her life. She didn't think something like this was worthy of a discussion?"

Hank shook his head and rolled over. After knowing Edna for thirty-five years, nothing his mother-in-law did surprised him.

"Weren't we talking about going there at the end of the month?" he asked in a groggy voice.

"We should have made definite plans!" Karen cried. "Then she wouldn't have sold the house so fast."

"You underestimate your mama," Hank replied.

There's no doubt about it, Karen thought as she handed the gate agent her boarding pass. My mother's going to put me in my grave.

"You have to check your carry-on bag," the agent informed her.

"But then it's not a carry-on bag," Karen answered as politely as she could.

The agent's face remained impassive. "We are a full flight. There is no further room for carry-on bags."

Karen shook her head. "I'm sorry but I have a lot of important papers in my bag. I can't risk losing them."

Ten minutes later, after tearful pleading, and almost risking arrest, Karen crammed her bag into an overhead bin and then squeezed into her middle seat. She put her computer bag under the seat in front of her, and fastened her seat belt. The guy on her right was snoring, the woman on her left was wearing strong perfume that was starting to give her a headache. Karen stared straight ahead.

Thoughts were racing through her head. She had so many questions. Who was the buyer? Who was running the garage sale? Edna sometimes hid money or jewelry then forgot where she put it. Who knows what might disappear today? What family heirlooms might go missing?

After the plane took off, Karen got out her laptop. She was glad that her flight had Internet access.

Quickly she searched to see if there was anything else online about the garage sale. What she didn't expect was to see her mother streaming live, standing with a reporter in the dining room.

Karen gasped at the sight of skulls on the dining room table. Is my mother truly crazy? she wondered. She must be. What else does she have on display?

As if hearing her baby girl's thoughts, Edna's voice came through the computer. "And we have so many other interesting items for sale . . ."

I can just imagine, Karen thought, bracing herself. But she wouldn't find out until she got off the plane.

Her battery went dead.

11

In his tiny office in an old building in the West Forties in Manhattan, Cleo's about-to-be ex-agent, seventy-three-year-old Ronnie Flake, was cleaning out his files, throwing out headshots that he'd collected for more than forty years. He had no idea what happened to most of these wannabes, but held on to the photos in case any of them hit it big or became involved in a scandal. That had happened once years ago. He'd made big bucks by selling the picture of a young woman whose claim to fame ended up being the fact that she dated a married politician to the *New York Post*. Cleo Paradise's headshot was in a place of honor on his desk. But lately she hadn't returned his calls.

Ronnie ran his hands through his shoulder-length gray hair. I wanted her to do the stalker movie because it was a job, he thought angrily. A job is a job. How could I have predicted she'd be nominated for an Academy Award for that other silly little movie? *My Super Super.* Please. I never had a super super. I never had an *okay* super. That flick came out of nowhere and was a huge success! I shouldn't have told Cleo the script was stupid. And I should never have told her I planned to retire. Talk about stupid! I open my big mouth about retirement the week before that dopey movie opens and breaks all box office records. Why,

———◆———

God? Why? Her contract with me runs out next week. She'll probably sign with a big agent the next day. Life's not fair. It's just not fair!

Ronnie turned on the old fan in the corner of his dusty office. I made a decent living, he thought as he tossed photo after photo into a garbage bag. I got actors work. I made them happy. Then I finally come across someone like Cleo Paradise, someone who's destined to be a star, and I blow it. But she had no gratitude! She was back in the New York area and didn't want to see me at all. She could have at least invited me down to that house she rented in New Jersey for a hot dog and a swim.

Disgusted, Ronnie threw the trash bag across the room. He went around, sat at his desk, and leaned down to open the little refrigerator against the wall. The ringing of the phone delayed his first nip of the day. He spun around and grabbed the receiver.

"Flake Agency."

"Dad?"

"Who else would it be?" Ronnie asked his forty-nine-year-old son, Horace.

"You don't have to be nasty," Horace answered. After trying out many professions, Horace now drove a livery cab.

"I'm not. I'm in a bad mood."

"Well, I've got something to tell you that's not going to make you very happy."

"Can it wait?"

"I don't think so."

"Then let's hear it."

"You know it irks me that Cleo Paradise has never appreciated you."

"Yes, son, I do."

"As your son, it breaks my heart that you're making yourself sick over it. Breaks it into tiny pieces."

"Thank you." Ronnie leaned down and pulled a bottle of vodka out of the fridge.

"Well, every day I look online to see if there is something new about her."

"I often do the same."

"Did you look today?"

"No. I've been too busy. I've had much too much to do."

"Well, she moved out of that house in Jersey."

"Yeah, so?"

"She left a note saying she was off to do a big movie."

Ronnie sprang up from his seat. "A big movie! She's still under contract with me."

"That's why this news couldn't wait. I couldn't find anything about any movie she's doing. The woman whose house she rented is having a garage sale today. Cleo left some of her stuff there and the woman is selling it."

"Cleo was thrifty. She made me account for every penny. Why would she leave things behind?"

"Beats me."

"Does this woman know where Cleo went to do this *big* movie?"

"I don't know. You want to go have a talk with this lady?"

"Yes, I do."

"You can get away?"

"Yes, I can."

"I figured as much. Come on downstairs. I'm right outside."

Ronnie hung up the phone. He took Cleo's picture, slammed it facedown on his desk, took one more gulp of vodka, then ran out the door.

12

Four attractive, young, apron-wearing women were stationed on Edna's front lawn, ready to collect her garage sale guests' money. Two security guards were standing near the gate where Scott's fiancée was giving out tickets. She was blond and pretty, and wholesome as apple pie. But she wasn't wearing an engagement ring.

Nora was introducing herself. "Hello, I'm a friend of Edna Frawley's daughter, Karen. Karen asked me to stop by and speak with Edna. Is she here?"

"Yes, she is. What is your name?"

"Nora Regan Reilly."

"The writer?"

"Yes."

"Oh, I love your books. My sister and I read them all the time."

"Thank you."

I don't believe this, Regan thought.

"My name is Jillian."

"Pleased to meet you, Jillian. And this is my daughter, Regan."

Jillian shook both their hands then called out to one of the girls on the lawn. "Dawn, would you bring these ladies inside to meet Mrs. Frawley? This is Nora Regan Reilly . . ."

I wish Jillian would accompany us, Regan thought. I'd love to ask her a few casual questions.

"Come on, ladies," Dawn called out cheerfully. They followed her up the steps and into the house. "Mrs. Frawley!" she yelled. "Mrs. Frawley!!!"

"Honey, please, shush," Edna yelled back. "I'm doing an interview that's live on the Internet."

"Sorry!" Dawn turned to Regan and Nora. "It'll be just a few minutes," she whispered.

"Do you work at many of these sales?" Regan whispered back.

"This is my first one. I'm really excited!"

"Your first?" Regan asked. "Is Jillian in charge here?"

"She and her partner, Jody. I think Jody's out back. They run these sales all over New Jersey."

"How great," Regan said. "How did you get the job?"

"My friend Yvonne called me last night. She was sick and asked me to fill in for her."

"I'm trying to convince one of my friends to get rid of stuff in her attic. Maybe I should talk to Jillian."

"You'll have to talk to Jody. Jillian just left."

"She did?" Regan asked, turning around and glancing out the window. One of the younger girls was now handing out the tickets. There was no sign of Jillian. "That was fast. Is she coming back?"

"I don't think so. They have another garage sale this afternoon. Mrs. Frawley called them at the last minute and really wanted to have her sale today. So Jody is running this sale," Dawn said in a singsong voice, "and Jillian the other."

I'll have to say hello to Jody, Regan thought.

13

For more than twenty years, Frankie Frawley had loved his life at sea. Every night he got to play the piano and belt out a tune or two or three. Whatever songs were requested, Frankie sang. If he didn't know the words, he improvised. The crowd loved the handsome, personable entertainer, stuffing his tip jar until it overflowed. After his set he schmoozed with the audience, going from table to table, then retreated to the crew bar for a couple of pops. Sure, he would have liked a career like Billy Joel's, but no such luck. Frankie was paid to travel the world and sing, which wasn't so bad.

His life had once been like a Billy Joel song. He'd married his high school sweetheart when they were both nineteen and he was the lead singer in a popular local band. All the traveling and late nights didn't make for a conventional life, which was what Lorna wanted after the first few years of fun. After their divorce he swore he would never march down the aisle again. Eventually one of the band members got a nine-to-five job, another started college, and the group went kaput. But Frankie was determined to never give up his music. He found work singing at bars in Atlantic City. That was okay for a while, but he grew restless. An actor friend told him about a new cruise line that was holding auditions for singers in New York City. Frankie went to Manhattan, and after performing two songs was hired on the spot. He'd been sailing the seven seas ever since. Ten years ago he'd landed a spot on the ship of his dreams. It was a most prestigious cruise line but the staff and guests were not too stuffy. The ocean was Frankie's mistress, and he was content.

But in the last year things had started to change. A new cruise director had been hired who seemed to have his own agenda. Frankie had the feeling his days could be numbered. He was thinking of looking for a job on another ship when Rhonda Schmidt walked into the lounge with three of her friends from college. They'd booked a cruise to celebrate their forty-fifth birthdays and spend a stretch of time together, time they hadn't shared since they all lived in the same dorm.

Rhonda had requested a Bruce Springsteen song. "I'm from New Jersey," she'd said, raising her glass.

"So am I," Frankie called back, with a wink. There was something about her. He was relieved to see she wasn't wearing a wedding ring.

Frankie had many shipboard romances over the years, but this one was different. He felt that he'd met his soul mate. She was funny and smart and, like him, had grown up at the Jersey Shore. The Jersey Shore that had nothing to do with a reality show but had everything to do with the simple pleasures, like hanging out at the beach, miniature golf, getting up early to watch the sunrise with your friends, that first kiss . . .

Rhonda was divorced, had two sons in college, and owned a successful restaurant in Asbury Park. Suddenly the thought of living on land didn't make Frankie shudder.

A month after they met, Rhonda booked another cruise to be with him. Then Frankie had a week off and they'd rendezvoused in London. Frankie hadn't mentioned the romance to his mother or sister. The last thing he needed was Edna driving up to check out Rhonda's restaurant. Two weeks ago Frankie had twelve hours free when his ship sailed into New York. He'd gone down to have lunch with Rhonda at her restaurant and meet her kids. The boys had been polite but reserved. They'll warm up to me, Frankie thought. It's got to be tough to meet your mother's boyfriend. And their parents had only been divorced for a year. Because his mother had built-in radar, and would probably see on the news that his ship was in New York, he told her he had to stay onboard for security reasons. He felt guilty, but he was in love.

Now that Frankie was back at sea, he knew he couldn't live without her. Rhonda, that is. Last night he'd called her and proposed. Crying, she'd said yes. Today the cruise director had happily accepted his resignation, saying his nephew was a wonderful singer and hopefully could fill in.

Frankie knew Edna would be happy. She'd been on the ship for two weeks last year and almost drove him crazy. People liked her, and *most* of her stories, but she never stopped for breath. When she walked down the gangplank the final time, Frankie was exhausted. But at least they'd had time to talk. Edna tried to convince him to come home and buy her house. "I'll sell it to you for a song," she'd said. "You'll never get a house like ours for such a low price. I'd like to move to a condo where there aren't so many steps. I'd like to be around more people. You know me. I like to talk."

"No, Mom," Frankie had said. "I'm a man of the sea. If you're willing to sell it so cheap, you'll find someone to buy the house."

Who knew how life could change? Now the time was right! He'd gladly buy the house from his mother. Rhonda loved the idea when he mentioned it on the phone. She'd been living in a small apartment since her divorce. The house would be perfect for them, with plenty of room for her boys, who would love the pool. Frankie would sing at the restaurant. Everything was falling into place for the next wonderful phase of his life.

Mom is going to be so surprised, Frankie thought. She'll be thrilled to finally sell me the house, see me get married, have me back home . . .

In his cabin, Frankie looked at his reflection in the mirror. He'd taken after his father with his dark hair, dark eyes, and olive skin. Adjusting the bow tie on his tuxedo, he smiled. It was almost time to go down and play a set while the first class passengers enjoyed cocktails before dinner. Tomorrow the ship would dock at Casablanca.

How appropriate, Frankie thought as he sat on his bed and picked up the phone. Casablanca is for lovers. I wish Rhonda could share it with me. A few minutes later the phone was ringing in the home that would soon belong to him and his bride. He never imagined he'd ever want to live there again, but now he felt as if it were calling out to him. Come back, Frankie. Start your new life here. It's time to come home . . .

The phone rang four times. Finally Edna answered in a breathless voice. "Hello."

"Hello, Mom. It's Frankie!" he said, his face beaming.

"Well, what a surprise," Edna answered. "But I can't talk now."

Frankie blinked. It was hardly the response he was expecting. "Is anything wrong?"

"No, but I have a lot of news. I sold the house and today I'm having a garage sale. They're about to open the gates to the crowd. There's a mob outside."

"What?" Frankie sputtered. "You sold the house? I wanted to buy it. Mom, I'm coming home. I'm getting married. I'll be back for good next week!"

"What's that expression? A day late and a dollar short? Call me back later. By the way, I've found love, too. Isn't it nice to find someone you want to spend your life with? I always told you not to be discouraged by your rotten experience with that self-centered ex-wife of yours. From the minute she didn't like the corsage I picked out for you to give her for the prom, I knew she was no good. I told you over and over. But like always, you didn't listen to your mama. Gotta go, Frankie."

The phone clicked in his ear. Frankie's heart was beating wildly. He called his sister's cell phone, but it went directly to voice mail. Then he tried her house in San Diego. Hank answered.

"I just heard about Mom selling the house," Frankie said, his mouth dry. "Is Karen there?"

"No, she's on a plane headed for Jersey. She got the news this morning. Karen's pretty upset, too." Hank tried to laugh. "You know Edna. She's always been impulsive. Maybe it will work out okay. Consider yourself lucky you're thousands of miles away and don't have to deal with it."

But I will have to deal with it, Frankie thought. I just quit my job and I have no place to go. No nice house a block from the beach with a pool and a big backyard for my new family.

My future stepsons will not be impressed.

14

As Regan and Nora waited in the vestibule, Edna's voice resonated throughout the house. "All these unusual objects were in a trunk in the garage. Yes, I suppose it is surprising that Cleo didn't bring them with her. What makes these things so interesting, aside from the fact that they look so crazy, is that they belonged to a sweet girl like Cleo Paradise. Don't you agree?"

"Absolutely! They give an interesting and unexpected insight into her personality. Who would have thought that these types of things would ever belong to her?"

I can't wait to see what they are, Regan thought, as she stepped closer to a framed letter on the wall.

"Cleo wrote that," Dawn whispered, her eyes dancing. "I love love love her. I put first dibs on her *My Super Super* T-shirt. Mrs. Frawley said I could have it, unless she gets someone who wants to pay her tons of money for it. I've got my fingers crossed!"

"Cleo received an Academy Award nomination for that movie. I'm surprised she wouldn't have wanted to keep the shirt."

"Mrs. Frawley found it under her bed."

Regan half smiled, then turned to read the letter. Nora had been staring out the window at the growing crowd. She walked over and joined Regan.

They silently read the scrawled note.

Dear Mrs. Frawley,

I loved staying in your beautiful home! I'm leaving early as I've been offered a part in an awesome new movie. I'm so sorry but I knocked over a vase, broke two wineglasses, and made a mess of your iron. I wanted to buy you a new one before I left but now I don't have time. OH! I also dropped your china teapot. Please keep the security deposit. I hope it covers the expense of replacing these items. If I left anything behind, please just throw it out or do what you want with it. I don't want to further inconvenience you.

Warmest wishes,
Cleo Paradise

Regan turned to her mother. They shared a knowing look, both wondering why Cleo was in such a hurry. The note gave Edna permission to sell what Cleo left, but clearly Cleo didn't think she'd forgotten much, if anything. And the note was obviously written in a great hurry on paper torn from a notebook. The bottom half of the white sheet was discolored, as if something had spilled on it.

The sudden loud ringing of the phone halted Edna's conversation with the reporter. "I'd better get that," she cried. "It could be my lawyer. Son, I hate to interrupt the interview. Can you turn off the camera?"

"That's okay. I'll do a commentary on Cleo's skulls and other items while you're on the phone. If it's Cleo Paradise calling, please let me know. It would be a real coup if I got to ask her a few questions."

Edna stopped dead in her tracks. If it's Cleo calling, she thought, I don't want to answer. What if she tells me she wants her belongings back? But if I don't answer now, I'll look bad. "I'll let you know if it's Cleo," Edna promised, running toward the kitchen.

Dawn whispered to Regan and Nora, "The second Mrs. Frawley gets off the phone, I'll tell her you're here. Be right back." She turned and walked toward the back of the house.

Nora and Regan looked at each other. "Skulls?" they both mouthed.

Edna's conversation must have been brief. Within seconds they heard her scream, "Nora Regan Reilly is here! In the house? Honey, you should have told me immediately. Nora!"

Edna's heavy-footed approach drew Nora and Regan to the entrance of the dining room. As they reached the doorway, Edna appeared from the other side of the room. The sight of Edna in her sixties flower power jumpsuit stimulated a frightening flashback in Nora's brain. She'd seen that jumpsuit decades ago, when Edna picked Karen and Nora up at a beach club teen night two hours early and decided to join the kids on the dance floor.

"Nora!" Edna cried again. "It's been so long! I have a pile of your books for sale out on the back lawn."

Nora managed a genuine smile as she opened her arms. "How wonderful."

Edna reached Nora and gave her a crushing embrace. "If you sign the books, I'll get more money for them."

"How wonderful," Nora repeated.

Edna looked into Nora's eyes and squeezed Nora's forearms so hard that Nora flinched. "Karen told me you two got friendly again." Squeeze squeeze.

"Yes, we did. She called me this morning and mentioned the sale," Nora said delicately. "Edna, I'd like to introduce you to my daughter, Regan."

"Hello, Regan!" Edna reached for Regan's hand and pumped it with vigor. "Karen tells me you're a private investigator."

"Yes," Regan said as she realized the reporter was zooming his video camera in on her face. "It's so lovely to meet you."

One of the many people watching the interview was Scott. He glanced around his office nervously. He was sure that he had seen that private investigator before. A pit formed in his stomach when he realized she had been at the restaurant last night. He had seen her clearly from where he was sitting. Quickly he picked up the phone and called Jillian.

She answered after three rings. "Where are you?" he sputtered.

"In the car."

"Did you see that author Nora Regan Reilly and her daughter when they showed up at Frawley's place?"

"Yes."

"Did she recognize you?"

"What do you mean?"

"The daughter was at the restaurant last night."

"She was? I didn't see her."

"Your back was to her. She definitely saw us. Her name is Regan Reilly and she's a private investigator. Don't go back to the house. The last thing we need is her asking questions."

15

I'm getting log cabin fever, Cleo thought. Maybe I'll go for a walk. She went into the rustic-looking yet thankfully modern bathroom and took a long shower. When she turned off the water she wrapped herself in a towel. After combing her hair and applying her face and body creams, she walked through the living room and up the flight of steps to the sleeping loft.

Daisy better get here soon, she thought, rummaging through the drawers. I'm running out of clean clothes. The duds I left at Frawley's are probably being picked over right now. I should have checked the house more carefully when I packed up, but I was terrified. I couldn't stay there one more minute. I probably should have finally called the police but I couldn't bear any more crazy publicity. Who would leave a letter like that? Only someone deranged.

I want people to forget that lousy film, she thought, as she eyed her running shorts. I don't need to give it any more attention. I'll never get another decent part if that image of the stalker victim follows me. As it is all the scripts I've been sent lately are garbage. And I'm not going to sign on for another role until my contract with Flakey is up.

Feeling more lonely and anxious than ever, Cleo decided to

go for a run. She quickly dressed in her running clothes, put on her socks and sneakers, then descended the stairs. She was tempted to look at her computer for any updates on Edna's sale, but decided she couldn't bear to read another word about it.

For a few minutes Cleo did stretches, trying to get the kinks out of her legs. I hate it when I don't work out for several days. I really feel the difference. Doing laps at Edna's pool was great exercise, she thought as she tucked her hair under a baseball cap, grabbed her oversized sunglasses, opened the cabin door, and stepped outside. The air was hot. A gnat buzzed around her ear. She brushed it away and started to run up a steep trail into the woods. This is hard, she thought. The air was heavy. But she forced herself to keep going. For thirty minutes she ran, following the narrow path up into the hills and back down. In the distance, through the trees, she caught glimpses of the lake. She slowed down when she approached a couple coming from the other direction, walking with a little girl who looked as if she were four or five years old. The girl was carrying wildflowers. She smiled at Cleo.

"Look what I picked!"

"Beautiful," Cleo said, but kept going. At least they're not dead, Cleo thought as sweat poured down her face. She was almost back to her cabin. I can't wait to get a glass of cool water, she thought. Maybe I'll even go down to the lake and find a private area to swim. I can't believe I showered before I went running.

She ran past the back of her cabin, rounded the corner, stopped short, and gasped.

Tall, broad-shouldered, Dirk Tapper was standing in front of her door. "Hey there, little lady," he said, with an easy grin on his face. "I was just about to go back down the hill. It's nice to see you're finally enjoying our beautiful facilities. It's about time."

Cleo was trying to catch her breath. She wanted to go inside but he was blocking the way. "Yes," she said, huffing. "The trails are beautiful."

"How did you like the lake?"

"It looked great. What I could see of it from the woods."

"You haven't been swimming?"

Cleo looked puzzled. "No."

"Don't look at me like I'm crazy," Dirk said. "What gave me a clue was your bathing suit."

This guy is cute, even really cute, but I don't know what to make of him, Cleo thought. "I'm not wearing a bathing suit," she said evenly.

Tapper started to laugh, slapping his knee several times. He was wearing boots and jeans even though it felt like it was a thousand degrees out. "You're funny," he finally said. "Do you think I'm as dumb as I look?"

Cleo shook her head. "No, I mean . . ."

"So you do think I look dumb."

"No I don't," Cleo said, slightly flustered. This guy lives his life like he's in an old Western. And he reminds me of a young John Wayne, she thought.

"I'm just teasing you, sweetheart. You're adorable. I wish you didn't spend all your time writing that meditation book. Don't you get lonely in there?"

Cleo shrugged. "I won't be doing it for much longer."

"Can I read what you've written so far?"

"I'll send you a copy when it's published."

He stared at her, grinning again. He put a toothpick in his mouth. "Your secrets are safe with me."

Is he putting me on? Cleo wondered. Does he know who I am? If he does, he's a better actor than I am. But he can tell I'm hiding something. "I'd better get back to work."

"You don't want to go for a cool dip first?" Dirk asked. "Our lake has got the cleanest water you've ever seen. I'm going for a quick swim. Why don't you join me? I promise I'll get you back up here in no time at all. Come on."

"I would but . . ."

"I'm not taking no for an answer," Dirk interrupted with a wave of his hand. He turned and walked around the corner of the other side of the cabin.

"What?" Cleo asked under her breath as she followed him. When she rounded the bend, she felt her knees go weak. Hanging on the clothesline was the bathing suit she knew she had left in Edna's pool house. How did it get there? How?

16

Daisy Harris was changing clothes in the crummy bathroom of a gas station, getting into the outfit she'd be wearing in her next scene. They weren't kidding when they said this would be low budget, Daisy thought. She was tired and sunburned but happy to be working. Her part was that of a waitress in a roadside diner in the middle of nowhere. A rambling kind of guy, unbelievably handsome, wanders in, and they end up falling in love. But because the course of true love never does run smooth, especially in a movie, his ex-girlfriend shows up at Daisy's isolated house in the middle of the night and tries to kill her.

Daisy was grateful the reshoots of that scene were over. April Dockton, the actress who played the ex-girlfriend, didn't have to do much acting for the part. She knew Daisy was Cleo's best friend. And the lead in *My Super Super* had almost gone to April. It had been down to the wire, with Cleo and April being called back several times. The director finally chose Cleo, the movie was a hit, and Cleo was a star. Not that she didn't have her troubles, thanks to the stalker movie, but she was a star.

April was still struggling. And unless she somehow landed a role as famous as Scarlett O'Hara, she'd never get over it. She could barely disguise her disdain for Cleo. Daisy was guilty by association. Which didn't make for pleasant chitchat between takes. What it did make for was a totally believable scene when April had to wrap her hands around Daisy's throat and scream like a maniac. Daisy was relieved that scene had been shot first, and April was gone.

Daisy was ready to go home. I just hope we finish these reshoots by tomorrow, she thought. Poor Cleo is waiting for me to drive back cross-country with her. If only she'd get another part like she had in *My Super Super.* April could never have done justice to that role. Cleo adopted some of the mannerisms of the super at her apartment complex in L.A. to hilarious effect in the film.

There was a knock at the door. "Daisy, are you ready?" one of the production assistants called.

"Be right out." Daisy looked at her reflection in the cracked, dirty mirror. A dingy lightbulb hung overhead. "Ugh," Daisy mumbled as she fluffed her dark brown hair. "Lighting is everything."

Like Cleo, she was twenty-four. They'd met in acting class, done a scene together, and hit it off immediately. And now we're both working actors, Daisy thought. Cleo is famous but she's still the same Cleo.

It would be so perfect if we were in a film together, Daisy thought as she grabbed a tissue from her purse and used it to open the door. No way I'm touching that handle.

Daisy stepped outside and got into the jalopy that was used to transport anyone on the film who needed a ride. The next scene was taking place down the dusty highway where she and her new love are stranded with a flat tire.

The driver of the car was an eighteen-year-old boy named Zeke who was mad about Cleo Paradise. He never stopped asking Daisy about her. But Daisy didn't mind. She was proud of her friend.

They started to pull out of the station.

"Your friend," the kid began.

"Cleo?" Daisy asked somewhat amused.

"What movie is she doing now?"

"She's not doing a movie now," Daisy answered.

"Yes she is. I just read it on my BlackBerry. But nobody seems to know much about it."

Daisy shook her head. "No. You must be mistaken. I just talked to Cleo Monday night. She's in New Jersey at a house she rented, waiting for me to join her. We're going to drive back to California together."

The kid shrugged. "Some lady's having a garage sale and is selling some of Cleo's stuff. Cleo had stayed at her house or something. Cleo's not there anymore."

"She's selling Cleo's things?"

"Her clothes."

Daisy felt stricken. Wouldn't Cleo have told her if she'd gone to do a movie?

"Here you go," Zeke said as he stopped in the middle of the highway, deserted except for the camera crew.

"Thanks." Daisy got out of the car. She was dying to contact Cleo. But the director was ready to start, and all the reshoots had made him crabby. She'd have to wait until the scene was finished.

Which could take hours.

17

Scott loosened his tie. Sweat broke out on his forehead even though the air conditioner was on full blast.

He rented office space in a commercial building in Paramus. Graduating with a degree in accounting fifteen years ago, he'd spent ten years working as a CPA for a large firm until they downsized, and he was let go. He opened up his own one-man operation shortly afterward. It wasn't easy making ends meet.

The phone on his desk rang. He glanced at the name on the caller ID. Summoning nerves of steel, he picked up the phone.

"Hello."

"Scottie boy."

"Yes, hi."

"You were going to pay me a visit last night. What happened? I thought you planned to come by and say hello."

"I need a little more time."

"That's what you said last week."

"I know. But I promise I'll get the money to you by Monday." Scott's voice was tight.

"Well, I hope so. The interest is skyrocketing."

"Don't worry."

"What, me worry?" the caller said ominously.

There was a knock on Scott's door. "I've got to go," he said. "I'll be in touch."

"So will I."

The phone clicked in Scott's ear. He replaced the receiver and called, "Come in."

The door opened and Barney, one of the guys who worked in a law firm down the hall, stepped into the room. "Hey, Scott, you want to grab some lunch?" Barney asked. "Not that I need it," he added, patting his stomach. "My wife's on my case about losing weight so she made me bring a salad to work. I ate it and I'm still hungry. I'd love to grab a burger. Besides, I feel like getting out of here for a while."

"I understand," Scott said, standing up and grabbing his jacket. "But I'm sorry I can't have lunch. I have a meeting."

"You all right?" Barney asked.

"Yeah, sure."

"Trevor okay?"

"Yes. He's up in Maine with his mother." Scott tried to laugh. "And his rich stepfather."

Pushing his glasses back on his nose, Barney looked at Scott with sympathy. "It's tough," he said as he shook his head, his toupee in danger of shifting. "But, man, if I were single and had your looks, I'd be out on the town every night. You'll have no trouble finding a rich stepmother for Trevor."

Scott reached for his keys and his cell phone. "That's the furthest thing from my mind right now. Getting my life on track after the divorce hasn't been easy."

Barney shifted from foot to foot. "You around this weekend? Tina and I are having a barbecue on Saturday. There will be a lot of kids running around, but it'll be fun. Tina's brother is coming in from Chicago. He's a really interesting guy." Barney whistled. "I wish I had his money."

"Can I let you know?"

"Sure. You can decide on Saturday if you want."

Together they walked out into the parking lot. Cars were whizzing by on Route 17.

"See you later," Barney said with a wave as he walked toward his car.

Scott opened the door of his leased BMW and got inside. The air was stifling and the seat was hot. He turned on the car and the air conditioning, then rolled down the windows. The cell phone in his pocket started to ring. It was Jillian.

"What's going on?" he asked.

"I just called Jody," she said quickly. "She couldn't talk because she was being introduced to that Regan Reilly and her mother."

18

Don't let us stop your interview," Nora said to Edna. "We'll wait."

Edna turned to the reporter. "This isn't a reality show. How much longer do you need me?"

"Do you have any more of Cleo's items?" he asked.

"In the living room. Follow me. Come on, Nora. Regan."

Regan had barely had time to absorb the collection of painted skulls, obviously artificial, and vases decorated with crazy faces. She followed her mother into the living room.

The room was large, with beautiful, if fading, yellow print couches, a floral rug, rattan end tables and ceramic lamps. There was a price tag on everything.

A rack of clothes and a card table seemed out of place in the middle of the room.

"I thought Cleo's clothes should be displayed in the most elegant room in my house," Edna said.

A few pairs of designer jeans, lighter summer pants, shorts, and T-shirts hung on a rack.

"And then," Edna said, pointing her manicured hand to the card table, "here are a few other items people might enjoy." She held up a pair of sandals. "What girl wouldn't want to walk in Cleo's shoes?"

Someone who doesn't wear the same size, Regan thought.

"And here is her pen, her lipstick, her suntan lotion, three notecards with 'Cleo' engraved on them, three matching envelopes included, a comb, a brush, and a beach towel from Malibu. Any fan of Cleo's would love to have these items, which might become more and more valuable as the years go on. Who knows? Cleo Paradise could be her generation's Meryl Streep." She turned to the reporter. "Mark, would you like to have a quick tour of the house to see the things of mine that are for sale? I have more beautiful furniture. I mean, I won't kid you. None of them are antiques, but they look good, and they're priced to sell."

"No thank you, ma'am," Mark said quickly. "I'll go out and talk to people in line."

"Be my guest."

The reporter waved as he panned the living room with his camera, then disappeared into the vestibule and out the front door.

"He was sweet," Edna said. "But enough's enough. I doubt anyone is watching that report. I don't want to waste my time and I'd rather catch up with you, Nora. It's so good to see you again. I heard you finally bought a house down here. I hope we'll see more of one another." Once again she squeezed Nora's arms. "And, Regan, it's lovely to meet you." Edna laughed. "You're a private investigator. Did Karen send you over to see if I had lost my marbles? She's jetting her way East as we speak."

"No," Nora laughed. "Though she does feel badly about the house being sold."

Edna shrugged. "She'll get over it."

"Who did you sell the house to?" Regan asked.

"A young man who works on Wall Street and wanted a house in Bay Head. His wife is pregnant and he wants to buy it for her as a surprise. She's due in the next week. I asked if he wanted to buy any of the furniture but he said no. His wife likes modern. So I'll get rid of whatever I can. I'm downsizing."

"Where are you going to live?" Regan asked.

"Golden Peaks. It's a retirement village nearby. There's a sweet little unit that I will furnish simply." Edna clapped her hands. "Would you like a cool drink? We could sit in the kitchen until someone comes and hopefully buys the chairs we're sitting in."

"Well," Nora said. "If it doesn't inconvenience you . . ."

"Not at all," Edna said. "Is there anything you'd like to buy first?"

"Oh, I'd rather visit with you," Nora answered tactfully. "We'll look around later. Are you sure you don't want to see what's going on outside?"

Edna waved her hand. "No. That's why I hired a company to run the sale. They know what they're doing."

"How did you find them?" Regan asked, dying for information on Jillian.

"Talking about me?" a woman called.

They all turned. A thin, dark-haired woman, probably in her late thirties, was walking into the living room. "I'm Jody," she said with an air of efficiency. "We put flyers all over. Edna saw me putting one up in the coffee shop in town, and asked what I was doing. Right, Edna?"

Edna nodded. "Monday morning. It was fate."

"Sure was," Jody said. "Edna put us right to work. She wanted to have this sale as fast as possible. We've been working round the clock this week . . ."

Not Jillian, Regan thought. She had time to go to a Chinese restaurant last night.

"And Jody is so good on pricing things. I wouldn't know what to charge. She kept saying get as much as you can . . ."

"Edna!" Jody protested.

"Well, that's your job. I don't want to give all this away. Jody, we're going in the kitchen for a drink. I know you don't have time to join us."

"Hardly," Jody said, looking at her watch. "I'd better see what's going on outside. It was nice to meet you . . ."

Edna slapped her forehead. "Forgive me for being rude. Let me introduce you to the author Nora Regan Reilly, who stayed in this house many, many, many times as a teenager. . . ."

I don't think it was that many, Regan mused.

". . . they had such a wonderful time. My daughter Karen and Nora went to high school together in Bernardsville. This was our summer place back then. Karen will be here tonight. And this is Nora's daughter, Regan . . ."

19

———◆———

Edna's friend Arnetta, a tiny woman with snow white hair and a heart-shaped face, was shooting pool in the recreation room at Golden Peaks. "Green ball in the side pocket," she announced with confidence as she leaned over the table and lined up a shiny wooden pool stick between her manicured fingers. She aimed, fired, and the sharp crackling sound of one ball hitting another filled the air. The players watched as the green ball rolled toward that side pocket, then began to run out of steam.

"Come on!" Arnetta cried, jumping up and down. The ball rolled more and more slowly, reached the edge of the pocket, then disappeared under the table with a decisive thump. "Yes!"

"You're a hustler, Arnie," one of the men said with a chuckle.

Eighty-six-year-old Arnetta was the best female pool player in the village. She'd taken up the game when she moved there ten years before. None of the women wanted to play with her anymore. She was out of their league and had gotten so competitive. Arnetta didn't care. She preferred playing with the guys who were the best. It was more fun and she loved to flirt.

A group of women who'd been playing cards on the other side of the room finished their game. One of them got up and walked over to the pool table.

"Arnetta, we promised Edna we'd take a ride over to her sale. Are you coming?"

"Nope."

"You're not?" Gladys asked.

"I don't want any of her junk. I've got enough of my own."

The men laughed.

Gladys put her hand on her hip. "We're not going over there to buy junk, Arnetta. We're going over there to show our support. I thought Edna was your friend."

"She is my friend. And I show her plenty of support. She's moving here because of me, isn't she? Maybe I'll drive over later and find out how much money she raked in. Not that she doesn't have enough already. She thinks she doesn't, but she does. Gladys, we're in the middle of a tournament . . ."

"Good-bye, Arnetta." Gladys turned away with a disgusted look. It's not nice the way that woman is always teasing Edna about money, she thought as she walked toward the door, where her friends were waiting.

"Arnetta's not joining us?" one of the women asked.

Gladys shook her head. "How did you guess, Margaret? She says they're in the middle of a tournament, but really, she can't be bothered."

"I knew she wouldn't want to join us," Margaret replied. She lowered her voice. "I don't think any of that group would admit it, but they're playing for money."

20

I'll get that," Cleo said, hurrying over to her bathing suit and pulling it off the clothesline. Her heart was beating wildly.

"So," Dirk said. "How about a swim?"

Cleo looked up at him. His face seemed kind. She didn't want to be by herself. "Might as well. You want to wait a minute while I put this on?"

Dirk pulled the toothpick out of his mouth and smiled. "I've got all the time in the world for you."

Oh, God, Cleo thought. Is he a nice guy or a nut? I don't know. Maybe I should just pack up and leave. But at this point I wouldn't know where to go. "I'll be right out."

Dirk nodded.

Cleo unlocked the door of the cabin, hurried inside, and shut the door harder than she intended. I hope he doesn't think I slammed it, she thought, breathing more heavily than when she stopped running. Who followed me here? Who? She went over to the desk where she'd left her cell phone and dialed Daisy, but it went directly to voice mail. Cleo hung up, hurried into the bathroom, and glanced in the mirror. Look at those bags under my eyes.

A sound behind the shower curtain startled her. She spun

around and yanked the curtain aside. The faucet was dripping. Cleo ran out of the bathroom and up the stairs to the loft. She checked the closet. No one was there.

Okay, she thought. I'll go swimming with Dirk. Maybe that will clear my head. Then I'll figure out what to do. She went downstairs again, changed into her suit, looked for her beach towel, and realized she didn't have it. Cleo put on a T-shirt, stuffed her feet into a pair of sandals, grabbed her sunglasses and cap, and went outside.

"Taking a swim in the lake always calms me," Dirk said gently as they started walking down the trail together.

I don't think anything will calm me, Cleo thought. "Swimming is great exercise," she said, her voice sounding hollow.

"I just have to stop at the office for a second and change into my bathing suit," Dirk said. "Don't worry. It's not a Speedo."

Oh, God, Cleo thought.

They reached the office, which was next to the parking lot where the campers left their cars. Cleo's rented SUV was parked in the corner. When people checked in, a golf cart brought guests and their "gear" up to their cabins.

"I'll wait outside," Cleo said. "I've been inside so much . . ."

"Okay. I'll be back in two shakes."

Cleo waited. The air was so quiet and peaceful. I'd love to be here under different circumstances, she thought.

Inside the office, Dirk greeted Gordy. "You're back."

"Yes," Gordy said eagerly. "It didn't take long."

"That's good," Dirk said as he walked back to his private office. "I'm going for a swim with Camper Long. She finally decided to come out of her shell."

"Great! When I came back I parked next to her car and noticed a bathing suit on the ground under the back door. It was hard to see because it's green and kind of blended in with the grass. Anyway, I took it up to her cabin but she wasn't there so I hung it on her clothesline." He smiled. "I'm trying, boss!"

"I'm proud of you, Gordy."

Dirk was puzzled. If Camper Long didn't put her suit on the clothesline, why didn't she say anything to me? Wouldn't she want to know how it got there? No wonder she seems nervous. What's up with her? "I'll mention it to her, Gordy," Dirk lied. "But don't you say anything. I don't want her to think we're fishing for compliments."

21

Hayley was seated at a prime table in Redman's, a trendy restaurant in the theater district, with Laurinda Black. Laurinda was in her late forties and had produced several successful off-Broadway shows. *The Tides Return* would be her first foray on the Great White Way. She was dressed casually, as if she had just run over from the theater, which she had. Black top, jeans, curly hair, not much makeup, glasses on a chain around her neck, Laurinda had the look of someone who knew that she didn't have to get dressed up, even at a place like Redman's.

Laurinda tore at a piece of bread. "Hayley, congratulations. I've been hearing all good things about the premiere last night."

"Thank you," Hayley answered.

"The movie opens in theaters tomorrow?"

"Yes."

Laurinda popped the bread in her mouth. "I've heard it's not that great."

You're not going to get me to say anything negative about a

client, Hayley thought. "Unfortunately I never get to watch the movie at these events. I'm too busy."

Laurinda nodded. "Gotcha." She ran her fingers through her curly brown hair that was flecked with gray. "We're still working on the script of our show. It's going to be great. It just needs a little bit of tweaking."

"With a new play, I imagine there could be revisions made right up until opening night," Hayley said cheerfully.

"Next time I'll do a revival of a classic. You can't make changes." Laurinda sipped her sparkling water. "You have much trouble with people crashing your parties?"

"No," Hayley replied quickly. "We make sure to have enough people working the door. If your name's not on the list, you don't get in. What I hate dealing with is all the people who call in the days before a big event, trying to weasel an invitation." Like Scott, she thought.

"I'm sure that happens a lot." Laurinda tapped the table. "When I first started in this business, there was a guy who crashed parties all over town and got away with it. He was harmless and just wanted to have fun. But now there are so many phonies and wannabes out there trying to get ahead. They go to these things to make connections, see what they can get from people they meet." Laurinda looked around. "A wealthy friend of mine was taken in by a guy she met at a fund-raiser. He was really handsome and asked her out. He took her to his favorite restaurant, where the waiters fell all over him. Turns out all he wanted was to invest her money."

"Really?" Hayley asked.

Laurinda started laughing. "She said she had to go to the ladies' room, right before their meal was served. Then she snuck out of the restaurant and sat in a bar across the street watching him sit with his meal and a cover over hers. Eventually he got the check, and she got the last laugh."

"Good for her!" Hayley said.

"Yup." Laurinda picked up her knife and playfully pointed it at Hayley. "I don't want anyone like that at my party."

22

. . . And this is Nora's daughter, Regan—"

Edna was interrupted by the ringing of Jody's cell phone. Jody smiled and looked down at her caller ID. "Excuse me for a second. It's Jillian, my partner in this crazy business . . . Hello . . . Yes, Jillian . . . You wouldn't believe who I'm meeting . . . Nora Regan Reilly, the author . . . Yes, and her daughter . . . Oh, you met them outside? . . . Listen, can I call you back? . . ."

Regan was staring at Jody as she listened to whatever Jillian was saying. What was that expression that crossed Jody's face ever so briefly?

"Okay . . . Hope it goes well . . . Talk to you later." Jody disconnected her phone. "Sorry," she said. "It's a busy day for us. Two sales at once."

"We met Jillian at the gate," Regan said casually.

"Jody and Jillian are so wonderful," Edna interrupted. "What a team! They taught me the value of decluttering and that's some lesson. It was like having two therapists for the price of one. Too much stuff keeps you stuck in the past. When I didn't think I could part with something, the girls told me to let go. I said I'd try. It wasn't easy. They told me to close my eyes and envision myself enjoying a new, wonderful life at Golden Peaks.

Clutter free. I followed their advice and now I'm ready to move forward."

"So many people have clutter issues," Regan offered. Like Scott, she thought. Too many girlfriends. "It's in the news all the time," Regan continued. "You're lucky to at least try and make money off your clutter."

"Oh, no!" Edna said. "What you see here isn't clutter!"

"Oh, what I . . . ," Regan began.

"We threw the clutter out! We went through the attic, the garage, and the basement. You think there's a lot of stuff outside? You wouldn't believe what I got rid of! Jody and Jillian said a sale like this must be staged properly. If you have too much garbage around, people will think everything is garbage and walk away. Right, Jody?"

Jody smiled. "Something like that." She looked at Nora and Regan. "Edna has so many beautiful things for sale. She doesn't need to try and make money on a chipped serving plate." Jody shuddered. "It gives people the wrong impression. We don't want anyone to get the idea she doesn't take care of her things."

"Which couldn't be further from the truth," Edna insisted.

"I could tell immediately," Jody said, looking at Edna with affection. "You have a beautiful home. But some of the stuff in your attic!" she joked.

"I have a sentimental streak a mile wide," Edna explained to the Reillys.

"Mrs. Frawley wanted to keep her son's first baby shoes. They were scuffed and curled up. A shoelace was missing."

"Frankie was a very active child. Always tapping his feet. No wonder he became a musician. Maybe I shouldn't have thrown those shoes out. He's moving back."

"He is?" Jody asked. "I thought he was married to the sea."

"He found someone else to marry. I can't wait to meet her. He just called a few minutes ago."

"Frankie's coming back?" Nora exclaimed. "You must be so pleased."

"Let's see if it happens."

"I'd better get outside," Jody said. "We'll start to let people in soon. One of our girls just went upstairs to keep an eye on the bedrooms. I'll be back in a few minutes to collect the money from people who buy things that are in the house."

"My daughter's bedroom door has a sign saying KEEP OUT?" Edna asked.

"Definitely."

Edna rolled her eyes. "Karen seems to think that every little thing from her childhood should be saved. She needs a crash course from Jody and Jillian."

Jody hurried outside.

Edna rubbed her hands together. "Ladies, how about a glass of iced tea?"

"Great," Nora answered.

I want to get a look around. Maybe I can get some information from the girl upstairs, Regan thought. "If you don't mind," she said to Edna, "I'd love to see the second floor."

"Of course," Edna answered happily. "Are you interested in bedroom furniture?"

"My husband and I renovated a loft after we were married last year. We still need odds and ends."

Nora started to say something then stopped herself. She realized her daughter would want to snoop around.

"We'll be in the kitchen," Edna said. "Go right up the steps."

"Thank you." Regan turned and went back to the vestibule. This is a beautiful home, she thought as she grabbed the banister and ascended the sweeping staircase. On her right was a collection of beach watercolors, all with price tags. The prices seemed reasonable.

A young girl was standing in the upstairs hallway. She looked about sixteen. "Hello," she said sweetly. "My name is Autumn."

"Hi, my name is Regan Reilly. My mother is a friend of Mrs. Frawley's daughter. I just thought I'd look around for a second."

"Sure. There are four bedrooms up here but one is off limits. The door is closed."

"Mrs. Frawley has lovely things," Regan said, making conversation.

"She does."

"I met Dawn downstairs. This is the first time she's worked at one of these sales. How about you?"

"My first, too."

"Really?"

"Yes. We're all new. Jillian and Jody do sales all over New Jersey. So they hire different kids for each sale."

"Makes sense," Regan answered. "Jody and Jillian are nice."

Autumn smiled. "Totally."

I don't think I'll get much more from her without looking like I'm fishing, Regan thought. "Which is the master bedroom?"

"The first door on the right."

When Regan stepped inside Edna's room and saw the unobstructed view of the ocean, she realized that this was the best room in the house. The bedroom was peaceful, decorated in peach tones. A flat-screen television hung on the wall.

Regan walked over to the window and looked out. She saw one of the security guards opening the gate. The first few people in line raced up the walk toward the house. It reminded Regan of the running of the bulls.

Turning away from the window, Regan surveyed the room,

then walked over to a steamer trunk that was sitting at the foot of the bed. It was for sale. She leaned down to take a closer look.

"That belonged to Cleo."

Regan looked up. Autumn was standing in the doorway.

"It's really nice. I'm surprised Cleo didn't take it with her."

Autumn shrugged.

"I thought Mrs. Frawley had all of Cleo's things together downstairs."

"She couldn't decide whether to sell the trunk until the last minute. Jody and Jillian said she might as well keep it up here since it looks good next to the bed."

Regan looked at the price tag. One hundred dollars. That's pretty good, she thought. "Autumn, I'd like to take this."

"Sure." Autumn walked over, and with a red pen wrote "SOLD" on the tag.

"Looks like you're going to be pretty busy with all the people still on line."

"Super-busy!"

A woman came darting into the room. "Look at that view!" she said. "It's fabulous! Oh, and that trunk! I just love it!"

"It's sold," Autumn informed her.

"Already? I was the third person on line."

"Oh, well, if you really . . . ," Regan began.

"Regan, it's yours," Autumn said. "Your mother's a friend of Mrs. Frawley."

"But I—," Regan began.

The other woman waved her hand. "Don't worry about it. I shouldn't even be here. My husband would have a conniption if he found out I'm at another garage sale." She disappeared out of the room.

23

Ready, Miss Long?" Dirk bellowed as he came out of the office. He'd changed into a pair of cargo swim trunks, T-shirt, and flip-flops. Like Cleo he was wearing a baseball cap and sunglasses. Two beach towels were under his arm.

Cleo jumped. She'd been staring into the distance, lost in her thoughts. "Yes," she answered. "By the way, you don't have to be so formal. Please call me Connie."

"Okay, Connie. Let's go."

Still flustered, Cleo blurted, "You have a little blob of suntan lotion on your cheek," she said, pointing with her finger.

"Oh. Nice," Dirk answered, obviously amused. He rubbed both sides of his face with his large, tanned hand. "How's that? Do I look presentable now?"

"Yes. Yes, you do," Cleo answered. Why did I tell him that? she wondered. I don't even know the guy. I'm so jumpy.

Silently they walked across the parking lot toward an opening in the woods. I wish I'd brought a bottle of water with me, Cleo thought. I'm so thirsty. I didn't even take one sip after my jog. For a couple seconds she debated internally whether to ask Dirk if they could go back to the office, then decided not to. Not after pointing out the lotion on his face. He didn't seem offended, but I should have kept my mouth shut. I don't want to bother him about something else.

For three or four minutes Cleo followed Dirk down a dirt trail completely shaded by overhanging trees. Just like the trail she had jogged on. Finally he stopped and turned. "I like to swim in a private spot off the beaten path," he said. "Do you mind?"

"No," Cleo answered quickly. Whoever left the bathing suit knows where I am, she kept thinking.

"It's probably not smart to swim in a secluded area since there isn't a lifeguard, but if I go under, I know you'll save me." Dirk rubbed his cheek. "I can tell you have my best interests at heart."

"You're a big guy, Dirk. I don't know whether I'd be able to save you, but I'll do my best."

"And I'll do my best to save you." He paused. "If you need it."

Dirk has no idea how ominous his words sound, Cleo thought. "Let's hope not," she answered.

Dirk turned and stepped off the trail into the woods, pushing branches aside. Twigs snapped beneath their feet. Talk about the path less traveled, Cleo thought as she followed him. A few minutes later the lake came into view.

"Careful, it starts to get a little steep here," he said, reaching for her hand. "Let me help you. I don't want you to slip and fall."

Cleo extended her arm and his hand closed around hers. She didn't expect it to feel so comforting.

"Easy does it," he said as the drop toward the lake got steeper and steeper. "Your hand is little, Miss Connie . . ."

Here we go with the Western stuff again, Cleo thought.

"Okay now. Going down this incline we have to be careful. It's easy to gain too much momentum . . ."

Their feet were moving quickly. They did gain momentum.

81

As they were about to reach the sliver of beach, the dirt started crumbling beneath their feet.

"Whoa," Dirk said as they tried to slow down. When they hit the beach, they couldn't stop, finally coming to a halt three steps into the water. Oddly exhilarated, they were both laughing. Dirk's other arm went around Cleo's waist to steady her. "Oops," he said as the beach towels started to slip from his grasp. He let go of Cleo and threw the towels onto the sand, followed by his shoes. He then pulled off his baseball cap, sunglasses, and T-shirt and tossed them on the heap. Cleo did the same.

Dirk smiled. "How about if I race you out to that marker? It's halfway across the lake. Can you make it?"

"Last one there is a rotten egg," Cleo said as she charged into the water.

"That's the spirit," Dirk whooped, diving under and swimming past her. The water's cold but refreshing, Cleo thought. It feels good to swim. I've been cooped up for too long. She swam every day at Edna's, except for the two days it rained. It's good to get this exercise again. She could see that Dirk was almost at the marker. He stopped, turned his head, and started to tread water. "You okay?"

"Yes," she called.

"Good." He turned and started swimming again.

A moment later, Cleo felt a slight cramp in her stomach. Then the pain got sharper. Oh no, she thought. I knew I should have had some water after that jog. I'd better go back. She started to turn her body but the pain was so great she doubled over and started to sink. Her mouth filled with water. Panicked, Cleo started thrashing her arms and legs. "Dirk," she tried to yell. If I go under, he'll never find me.

Dirk reached the marker and turned around. His expression turned to horror when he saw her struggling to stay afloat. "Connie!" he yelled, putting his head down and swimming toward her at a frantic pace. When he reached Cleo she was still thrashing her arms with surprising strength even though she felt exhausted.

"Easy, Connie!" Dirk shouted, attempting to grab her arm. But Cleo was in a panic. Her thrashing and flailing were primal. "Connie, stop!" Dirk ordered. "You have to let me help you! Relax! Float on your back!"

Cleo was terrified. But she had to trust him. She let herself go limp and put her head back. The cramp was gone, but so was her strength. Dirk put his right arm around her upper torso, rested her head on his shoulder, and with his left arm, started to paddle back to shore.

"Don't worry, Connie," he said gently. "You'll be fine."

On the beach, he eased her down onto the sand and placed the beach towel under her head. Cleo was breathing hard. "I'm sorry," she said, her chest heaving, her eyes filled with tears.

"No, I'm sorry," Dirk said. "I should never have left you like that. I didn't even ask you if you were a good swimmer. I could kick myself."

Cleo tried to smile. "I am a good swimmer. But I usually only swim in pools. I got a bad cramp. I was so afraid you'd never find me if I . . ."

Dirk's hand was on her cheek. "Relax, Connie. Just relax."

Cleo closed her eyes for a moment, then opened them again. "I'm okay. Let's get going."

"No."

"No?"

"You have to take a few minutes."

"Okay." Cleo closed her eyes again and tried to catch her breath.

Several minutes later Dirk helped her to her feet. Slowly they donned their shoes and T-shirts. Dirk took Cleo's hand and he started up the crumbling trail. But his right foot slid out of his flip-flop, and he started to lose his balance. He let go of Cleo's hand so he wouldn't pull her down with him. The last thing he wanted was to cause her more problems.

But it didn't work. She fell backward onto the beach.

24

Edna and Nora were seated at the kitchen table, glasses of iced tea in front of them. Nora had already autographed her books and they were back on the lawn in a more prominent spot.

"I can't believe all the years that have gone by," Edna said wistfully. "Remember how much fun we had, sitting at this table?"

Vaguely, Nora thought, as she smiled. "Of course, Mrs. Frawley. I had some very memorable moments in this house."

"Edna. Please, call me Edna. We're all grown-ups. Oh, I hear the front door opening." She grabbed Nora's arm. "Here we go! The sale's starting right now!" But then she wrinkled her nose. "What's all that yelling?" Edna pushed back her chair.

Nora and Edna hurried into the dining room, where a middle-aged man with a bad haircut and an ill-fitting shirt that barely covered his stomach was checking the price tags of the items on the table. "This all belonged to Cleo Paradise?" he was asking, sweating profusely. "All these painted skulls and pottery?"

"Yes," Jody answered.

"I'll take everything," he announced, gesturing broadly with his arms. He reached in his back pocket for his wallet. "I'm paying cash."

In the living room, a woman had her arms around the rack of Cleo's clothes. "This is all mine," she shouted. "I want everything here!"

Regan hurried downstairs when she heard the yelling. These people are crazy, she thought.

Another two women, most likely a mother and daughter, with the same bowl haircut, sharp nose, and square jaw, were clearly disappointed when they heard Cleo's things were sold out. So disappointed they started complaining in raised voices.

"Can't we buy one of the skulls?" they asked. "They're so different. We want a skull!"

Jody shrugged. "If this gentleman would be willing to—"

"No! I'm president of Cleo's fan club. This is all mine."

"But we were waiting in line for hours . . ."

"Oh, all right, I'll be nice. You can have one of them. Make your choice. Hurry up."

Regan had gone over to stand with Edna and Nora. For once, Edna was speechless.

The woman in the living room started throwing Cleo's former belongings into a clear plastic bag. "I'm not stealing anything," she yelled, almost to herself.

Are these two together? Regan wondered. They must be. She didn't have to wait long for an answer.

"Will you be buying anything else?" Jody asked the man, who was wiping his brow. "Or should I add this all up for you?"

"That's my wife in the other room. She's the vice president of Cleo's fan club. We're together. Honey!" he shouted. "In here! We'll pay this lady and hit the road."

What a pair, Regan thought. They must plan to resell this stuff on the Internet. They scooped up everything belonging to

Cleo. Except the trunk I'm buying. I guess I should join the fan club.

"Oh my," Edna murmured. "I never expected something like this would happen. Where are people's manners?"

Outside, word spread quickly that there was nothing left of Cleo's.

It started an uproar.

"After waiting this long!" some of Edna's garage sale guests shouted in disgust as they stomped away. "What a rip-off!"

A teenaged girl started crying. "I want to be an actress. I wanted something of Cleo's to inspire me!"

At least half the people in line left. Edna became distraught when she glanced through the window and saw the crowd disappearing. Like a shot she ran out the front door. "Come back, everyone! We have so many other lovely things that are still not sold . . . including signed copies of Nora Regan Reilly's books!"

Nora covered her ears.

25

Hayley and Laurinda were in the middle of their meal. Laurinda was eating her hamburger with gusto, but Hayley just picked at her salad. She didn't have much of an appetite. First she'd been reeling from Regan's news, then Scott's call really threw her for a loop. But she had to focus on the business at hand.

The restaurant was busy enough, but it was August, which for a place like Redman's meant fewer regulars. Most people in show business were out of town, many in the Hamptons. In September the crowds would be back and the place would be buzzing again.

Hayley was doing her best to be upbeat. "I was thinking that what we might do at your party was—"

Laurinda put her hand on Hayley's arm. "Just a minute," she said as she looked toward the entrance of the restaurant.

Hayley started to turn her head.

"No, don't," Laurinda said quickly, turning back to Hayley. Elbows on the table, she spoke into the side of her hand. "You can look, but don't make it obvious. I don't want that actress coming in to see me."

A middle-aged man and a striking woman in her twenties walked past, following the maitre d' to a private table in the corner.

Hayley stole a glance. She didn't want to admit it, but she had no idea who the actress was. And she felt it was her job to know all the famous faces. "Oh . . . ," she began, then decided she should be up front. As Laurinda said, there were enough phonies in the world. "I'm sorry, Laurinda, but I don't recognize her."

Laurinda's expression was blank as she looked into Hayley's eyes. "I like you, Hayley," she finally said. "You're honest."

Unlike that jerk Scott, Hayley thought. "Thank you."

"I mean it. There are people in this business who would have pretended they knew who she was. But the fact is, not many people do. Her name is April Dockton. She's done a few little films but nothing's clicked. She'd do anything to get her career going. That girl is scary."

"Really?"

Laurinda nodded. "She auditioned for my play but wasn't right. I kept hearing from her and hearing from her, she kept asking if she could audition again. She should play a stalker."

"Is she talented?" Hayley asked.

"She can act. But does she have that certain something that will make her stand out from all the other talented, beautiful young women her age? I don't know. What she needs is a lucky break."

Like me in the dating world, Hayley thought.

"All it takes is one . . ."

Yup, Hayley mused.

". . . one role in a movie or play that gets noticed."

Hayley nodded. "All it takes is one." She put down her fork.

"I love reading about unknown actors who made it really big after one role. Then you learn who turned down those very same parts, actors who had careers going, but never enjoyed the success they might have had if they had been smart enough to take that one role. It must be so hard to live that down."

"This business is full of coulda, shoulda, woulda. It's all about being able to judge what's a good script, what's going to be a good production." Laurinda's eyes darted in the direction of April Dockton, who was fawning over the man she was with, tossing her hair, smiling a little too happily, touching his arm. "She's working it," Laurinda murmured.

"What?" Hayley asked.

Laurinda tilted her head in April's direction. "That guy is a producer from the Coast who's about to get a movie going. Ten to one, there's a part in it April wants. She's ambitious, boy. You talked about people who didn't take certain parts and lived to regret it?" Laurinda asked, then paused for effect.

"Yes," Hayley said, waiting, knowing Laurinda was about to say something Hayley should find incredible.

"How about the people who come so close to a starring role and don't get it? They wanted it so bad they could taste it," Laurinda said, dramatically pointing to her mouth. "It was so close they could taste it!"

"That's got to be awful."

"Awful? I'll say it's awful! Especially for an unknown." Laurinda leaned in and whispered, "April Dockton was the second choice to play Cleo Paradise's role in *My Super Super.*"

Hayley's mouth dropped. She didn't have to fake her reaction to this tidbit. "She was?"

Laurinda nodded. "She almost nabbed it but in the end they picked Cleo."

"And Cleo became a star."

"That she did." Laurinda made a face. "I'll tell you something," she began, then laughed. "If I were Cleo Paradise, I wouldn't want to meet up with April Dockton in a dark alley. In any alley, for that matter."

26

Horace Flake was speeding down the Garden State Parkway, his father in the passenger seat.

"Son, slow down," Ronnie ordered, bracing his hand against the dashboard. "I want to get there in one piece."

"I drive for a living," Horace reminded his father. "Did you forget that?"

"You hang around the airport and try and get fares. Most people are afraid of gypsy cab drivers like you. They think they're going to get in your car and get murdered. That's not what I call driving for a living."

"Thanks," Horace said sarcastically, his thick, beefy hands gripping the wheel. "I'm so concerned about your welfare that I take the day off, and that's all you have to say? I want to see Cleo Paradise brought to justice. I want the world to know how she treated you. It's outrageous. You were her agent on a movie that lands her an Academy Award nomination, and now she's ignoring you."

Ronnie looked forlorn. "I told her it was a bad script." He shook his head. "I still think it was a bad script. A bad script that turned out good. Cleo worked her magic."

"I thought the stalker movie you got her was good," Horace

said, his hands gripping the wheel even tighter. "Now I watch the movie just to see the part where the guy tries to kill her. It's awesome."

Ronnie looked over at his son. Horace's dark hair was thinning. He had a big, strong frame but he had put on too much weight. All the junk food he ate while he was driving. Wrappers were scattered all over the floor. If only he'd get his life together. "Horace, I worry when you talk like that," he said. "Your problem has always been you like a fight. What's going to become of you when your mother and I aren't around? Huh? You ever think of that?"

"I live day by day."

"I'll say. You never got around to moving out."

"Mom didn't want me to."

"She changed her mind twenty years ago."

They rode in silence. "I'm sorry," Ronnie said. "But now that I'm going to retire, I worry. Your mom wants to move to Florida. Are you planning to come with us and try to snag fares at the Florida airports? It won't be easy. There won't be any long lines of people standing in the cold, tired of waiting for a legitimate taxi."

"You think I want to live in a retirement village in Florida?"

"Then what are you gonna do?"

"Stay here. I'll get a room somewhere. I'll figure it out."

Ronnie shook his head. "I should have been a better father."

"You're right." Horace put on his blinker and started steering his dark, beat-up sedan toward the exit.

"This is where we get off?" Ronnie asked.

"Yes."

"Then what?"

"I know the way," Horace said, quickly adding, "I got directions on my BlackBerry when I read about the sale."

27

C onnie, are you all right?" Dirk asked anxiously, as he got up off the ground. He winced at the pain in his ankle as he hurried toward her.

Cleo was staring straight up at the sky. "I feel a little dazed but I'm okay." She started to sit up. "This hasn't been my day."

"It's my fault again," Dirk said. "Take it easy, Connie. Are you seeing stars or anything?"

"I'm just a little foggy. No big deal."

"Relax for a few minutes, Connie." Dirk rubbed his ankle.

"Did you get hurt?" Cleo asked.

"I'll be fine. I might have a sprain. I'll go back and put some ice on it."

"Can you walk all the way back to the office?"

"My cabin is just a short ways up a path in the woods," he said. "When you're ready, I'll escort you back to the trail. Then if you don't mind, can you go the rest of the way by yourself?"

"I don't mind. And I'm okay now," Cleo said. "Let's go." Dirk took her hand and together they stood. But when they started to walk, he had trouble. It was painful to put weight on his foot.

"Lean on me," Cleo offered.

"Are you sure?"

Cleo smiled. "What do you mean am I sure? You just saved my life. I'll escort you to your cabin and get out the ice."

28

Cliff and Yaya Paradise were enjoying a glass of wine at their campsite.

"Ah," Cliff said, leaning back in his outdoor chair that folded up in a snap. "I love this mellow feeling when day is done, gone the sun. After the thrill of exploration, whether it be the excitement of climbing a mountain, or the challenge of learning a new dance step, there's nothing like sitting back and enjoying life." He grabbed his wife's hand and kissed it. "With my Yaya. The woman who never said no when I wanted to continue exploring Planet Earth. She only said ya . . . ya . . . Yaya!" He kissed her hand again.

Yaya smiled. "Till the day she died my mother could never get used to the nickname you gave me. But she loved to hear about our world travels."

"Our world travels meant getting a lot of painful shots over the years, but it was worth it," Cliff said, sipping the red wine they'd bought in the village. "What excites me now is the museum. Aren't we lucky to have come across those pottery skulls? They remind me of Mexican sugar skulls, but much easier to transport."

"I'll say," Yaya chuckled. "These last few months we really

found some interesting pieces." She paused, then put her finger to her temple. "I'm surprised Cleo didn't send us an e-mail when she received the trunk. She always opened the trunks we sent to Los Angeles right away and sent some funny comment. I received the confirmation the trunk was delivered to New Jersey. If she saw those crazy skulls, I can't imagine why we didn't hear from her . . ." Yaya's voice trailed off.

"Maybe she's gotten used to her crazy old parents. At least we know it arrived."

They sat in silence for a few minutes. "Cliff," Yaya finally said. "Why don't we go into town and call Cleo?"

"Now?"

"Yes."

"But why?"

"I want to hear her voice."

"Darling, can't you hear it tomorrow?"

"No."

Cliff looked at his wife. "What's the matter?"

"I don't know. Maybe it's a mother's intuition . . ."

"Say no more," Cliff said, draining his glass, then staring down into the valley. "We'll go down right now. On the one hand it's wonderful this campsite is removed from the modern world and the technology that has taken over so many people's lives, but on the other hand—" Suddenly he stopped talking. He turned to his wife.

Yaya was already running down the hill.

29

Regan turned to her mother and couldn't help but laugh as Edna boomed from the front porch, "Autographed books by the famous author Nora Regan Reilly . . ."

"Mom, don't worry about it."

"I know, Regan, but listen to her. It sounds like she's begging people to stay and buy my books."

The front door flew open. "Nora!" Edna called. "I have some-one here who wants to buy one of your books, but only if you're willing to personalize it—yes, or no?"

"Of course," Nora answered as sweetly as she could.

"Come on out here!" Edna ordered as the house phone started to ring. "Regan, would you get that, please? I'm very busy."

"Certainly." Regan and her mother exchanged looks of amusement, then headed in different directions. Regan hurried to the kitchen, where two women were examining the table and chairs. They seemed to be in a world of their own, and didn't notice the loud ringing of the phone, or Regan's presence in the room.

"It's a pretty nice table and a good price, but, eh, I've seen nicer."

Regan grabbed the cordless phone from the wall. "Frawley residence," she answered.

"Hello, is Cleo Paradise there?" a woman asked.

"No, she's not. Who's calling?"

"My name is Daisy Harris. I'm a good friend of Cleo's. When will she be back?"

"Actually," Regan said cautiously, "she's not living here anymore."

"She's not?" Daisy sounded surprised and a little upset.

"No, she's not."

"Where did she go?"

"I don't know," Regan responded. "I just answered the phone for the woman who owns the house. She's busy right now."

"I heard that woman is having some kind of sale where she's selling things that belong to Cleo. Is that true?" Daisy asked incredulously.

Regan felt embarrassed. "Yes, Mrs. Frawley is having a garage sale . . ."

"This is crazy!" Daisy exclaimed, sounding more and more upset. "Cleo wouldn't leave her things behind. When did she leave?"

"Last Friday, I believe," Regan answered. "She left Mrs. Frawley a note saying she was off to do a movie."

"A movie! But I just talked to her Monday night. She didn't tell me anything about a movie or that she had moved out of the house. She was waiting for me to finish work on a film I'm doing in Florida and then we were going to drive back to California together."

I knew it, Regan thought. I had the feeling that there was something odd about Cleo's sudden departure. "Maybe she's nearby and just wanted to leave this house for some reason," Regan suggested, in an attempt to comfort Daisy.

"Then why wouldn't she tell me?" Daisy asked, her voice rising. "Why?"

"When you talked to her the other day, was she on her cell phone?"

"Yes. I tried calling it just now but there's no answer. I left a message."

"I'm sure she'll call you back."

"No. There's something wrong. Cleo told me someone left wilted roses for her at that house. That happened in California, too. Both times she tried to shrug it off. She'd been in a movie about a stalker who left her wilted roses and figured it was just a prank. I have a bad feeling that it wasn't a prank this time."

I do, too, Regan thought. I do, too.

30

I hope Cleo Paradise is enjoying her day.
   Because it's her last.

31

———◆———

Scott shouldn't worry so much, Jillian thought as she drove her Jeep toward Asbury Park. So what if that Regan Reilly recognized me and starts asking questions? Jody will know how to handle it. And the girls working at the sale don't even know us, for goodness' sake, so they can't give her any dirt. It will all be fine. Besides, what does Regan Reilly care if I got engaged or not?

For the past twenty-six years, Jillian's mother had praised her daughter for having such a sunny outlook on life. As a baby, Jillian was always smiling and clapping her hands. As she got older, she always saw the glass as half full. Many people found her saccharine ways annoying. But there was no doubt that when life got tough, Jillian muddled her way through. You're right Mom, Jillian thought, happily. I do look on the bright side. But I also work hard. Jody would never have asked me to go into business with her if I didn't. She's a little older and more experienced, but she couldn't do this alone. She's better at pricing the items and I'm better at getting rid of the clutter. I've always been very neat. That's another of my good qualities.

Turning up the radio, Jillian listened as a reporter raved about the weekend weather forecast—beautiful and sunny. I wish I could go to the beach, Jillian thought, but we have those sales on Saturday and Sunday in Pennsylvania. Oh well. They'll be worth it. Both sales are at McMansions, which means we should make some good money; 25 percent of the take, as usual. Jody and Jillian were leaving early the next morning and would be gone for two nights.

I wonder how Edna's sale is going, Jillian thought as she zipped along Ocean Avenue. She asked if it would be better to have the sale on the weekend but we were already booked. Edna needn't have worried about having the sale on a weekday, she had quite a line. It's summertime and people are on vacation. Garage sales don't have to be just on Saturday or Sunday.

Jillian was nearing Asbury Park, a town that had always been an alluring place for musicians. It was home to the Stone Pony, a bar Bruce Springsteen performed at often in his early career. After years of decay Asbury Park was finally enjoying a slow but steady resurgence, thanks to building and renovation. New bars, restaurants, and lounges where musicians could perform had sprung up. I wouldn't mind living here, Jillian thought. The Perones seem to love it.

The Perones were the owners of the house where Jillian was headed. A couple in their early thirties, they were on a spiritual cleansing kick and believed that if they got rid of their junk, they'd be more creative and productive. Striker was a musician and Harriet worked in sales at a radio station. Jillian had helped Harriet go through the house, and had to be kind but firm, just like she was with Edna. People had a hard time letting go of their possessions.

The Perones' garage sale was beginning at 2:00. It was now 12:30. Plenty of time to assemble everything out on their patch of front lawn. No helpers needed. Jillian and Harriet and Striker would handle the sales themselves.

Jillian turned onto their street. The quiet block resembled a ghost town. The sun was beating down and there were few trees to provide shade. Even optimistic, glass-is-half-full Jillian felt a teensy bit nervous as she pulled down to the small house and turned into the tiny driveway. There were no people waiting out front. Jillian had posted signs in the morning all over town. There were always garage sale addicts who staked out a place in line hours before sales started, paranoid that they'd miss out on a good bargain. Some of them were downright scary.

Jillian wasn't even out of her car when a barefoot Striker came out the front door wearing his usual black jeans, black T-shirt, and an odd assortment of metal chains around his neck.

"Hi, Striker," Jillian said cheerily, thinking that he probably just rolled out of bed. Striker often played until the wee hours of the morning in bars around town. "Ready to stage our sale?"

Striker pointed his finger at her. "I have to talk to you," he said angrily.

Jillian closed her car door. "What's wrong?" she asked.

"What's wrong? Do you see any line? No one's going to bother coming here with that other sale going on—the one with Cleo Paradise's stuff. We booked you first for today and that sale is stealing all the attention! You wasted our time!"

"But that sale is several towns away. Believe me, the people there who know about yours will be here afterward. Definitely." Jillian smiled broadly. "I hung signs all over the place. Remember that movie *Field of Dreams*? If you build it, they will come. Believe me, if you have a garage sale, they will come!" Jillian started to laugh, a lilting, high-pitched ha ha ha.

Striker failed to find any humor in Jillian's little joke. "Not only that," he continued, his expression unchanged, "but Harriet let you throw out too much of my stuff! I'm furious!"

Jillian shook her head. "Oh, Striker," she said in a placating tone as she walked toward him. "It is so incredibly normal for you to feel that way. People have such a hard time letting go of their things. When the sale is over, you are going to be sooo happy. You are going to feel soooo free. Let's have a positive attitude, and get ready for your sale!" she said, doing her best to sound perky. "Where's Harriet?"

"She's in the house sobbing. She feels the same way."

32

My life is so messed up, Scott thought. I got married too young. Things were okay for a while, her parents helped us get started, then that witch always wanted more. She wanted to do nothing but shop, lunch with the girls, go on great vacations, join the most expensive country club. Then when Trevor came along she had to have a nanny and send him to private school. For a while I could swing it, then I lost my job. Things were never the same. I tried to keep up and we started fighting.

It was a relief when she met that rich old guy at the gym. When she told me she wanted a divorce, she thought I'd be heartbroken. Huh! What a joke. I just feel sorry that Trevor has a woman like that for a mother. He's stuck with her for life. I'm stuck dealing with her until Trevor graduates college.

Wouldn't it just kill her if she found out about the garage sale business? She'd die. Even though she liked the finer things in life, she stopped at those sales every week to get her fix. Sometimes she brought home something decent but mostly it was junk. The amount of money she wasted had driven Scott crazy and he told her as much.

Now he needed $25,000 and had to score it soon. I'll pay that guy back and never ever borrow again, Scott thought. Luckily I have this appointment today. An elderly couple who had been at the restaurant last night—Betty and Ed Binder—were so touched by the romance of Scott's proposal that they sent over a round of drinks. Good thing that Regan Reilly was gone by then. He was sure she was. Most of the restaurant had thinned out. Scott and Jillian thanked the Binders and asked the couple to join their table. Now Scott was going to pay them a visit. He had a few investments he wanted to talk to them about. Hopefully they'll get out their checkbook.

When he neared their gated community, he pulled over on a side street. He was early and didn't want to look anxious. He picked up his BlackBerry and did a search on Regan Reilly. He already knew that her mother was an author, thanks to that windbag Edna, streaming live on the Internet. He scrolled down for information. Her father owns three funeral homes in Summit, New Jersey? Scott chuckled. Good to know, he thought. But when he read who she was married to, his chuckles ceased.

Jack Reilly, head of the NYPD Major Case Squad.

They lived in New York City.

What were they doing at that Chinese restaurant in New Jersey last night?

33

D aisy, if you wait just a minute I'll get Mrs. Frawley. We can find out—"

"I can't wait," Daisy whispered into the phone. "I'm on the set. I shouldn't be talking on the phone. I have to go. We're about to shoot a scene."

"Let me take your number," Regan said quickly. "My name is Regan Reilly. I'm a private investigator. I'd like to help, if you can't reach Cleo."

"A private investigator!" Daisy said, alarm in her voice. "Did something happen you're not telling me?"

"No! My mother has known the Frawleys for years and we stopped by to say hello." That's true enough, Regan thought. She doesn't need the gory details about Edna.

"Okay," Daisy said, then quickly gave Regan her number. Regan grabbed a pen by the phone and scribbled on a message pad.

Regan repeated it aloud. "Would you like my number?"

"I don't have a pen. When you get a chance, would you please call my phone and leave your number on my voice mail?"

"I will. And don't worry, Daisy. If you just spoke to Cleo Monday—"

"I've got to hang up! Thanks. Sorry."

The phone clicked in Regan's ear. Slowly she replaced it in the receiver. This is too weird, Regan thought. Someone leaves Cleo dead flowers? Then she leaves early and doesn't tell her good friend? Why not? She must have been scared. Did whoever left the dead flowers follow her from this house?

People were passing through the airy kitchen and into the den where large windows overlooked the pool area and big, comfortable beige and white couches, another fireplace, and a large flat-screen television like the one in the bedroom gave the room a relaxed feeling. The curtains were open. If Cleo was scared, I'm sure she closed them at night, Regan thought. I want to walk around these rooms. Maybe something will give me a clue about Cleo's stay here or why she left. But probably nothing will. Cleo had been gone for nearly a week. Edna had been back and spent a few days preparing for the sale.

Regan walked into the dining room, where Cleo's fan club crazies were carefully packing up their goods. Jody looked a little aggravated as she added up their purchases with a calculator.

"So," Regan asked Mr. President and Madame Vice President. "How do you start a fan club?"

The guy shrugged and wiped his forehead. "You just do it."

The birdlike woman nodded, her eyes darting around the room. "You just do it."

"Are you in any other fan clubs?"

"Oh," Jody said in frustration, obviously directed at Regan. "I just lost track. I'm not sure if I counted that last skull. We'd better start over."

"Sorry," Regan said. "I'll get out of your way." She went through the living room and up the stairs again. Autumn was still there watching the shoppers who were going in and out of the bedrooms.

"A couple more people were asking about the trunk," Autumn said, her eyes twinkling. "But it's yours!"

Regan smiled. "Yes. I'm so glad about that. I want to look in those other bedrooms." She made a face. "I ran downstairs when I heard all that excitement before."

"Sure," Autumn said sweetly, no comment on the brouhaha.

The guest room was welcoming with a queen-sized bed, matching print curtains and bedspread, and a white desk, dresser, and end tables. Regan often wondered if people in guest rooms ever used the desk as anything other than a depository for their stuff. The other bedroom must have been Edna's son's room. A dark blue spread covered the twin bed. Framed photos of the Beatles and Rolling Stones hung on the walls, as well as the famous photo of a couple hugging in the middle of the crowded, muddy field at Woodstock.

A gray-haired couple walked into the room. The woman inhaled sharply. "Woodstock! Remember those days, honey? I wanted to go so badly but my father laid down the law. He wouldn't allow it! I was heartbroken. If I had been eighteen, I would have gone. I was born six months too late to be a part of history."

The man jutted out his lower lip and squinted as he looked at the photo. "You were lucky. Look at all that mud."

The woman rolled her eyes and winked at Regan. Regan smiled and walked out of the room. Time marches on, she thought. That woman looked so settled. It was hard to imagine she was the type who ever wanted to go to a rock concert.

Regan went back to the master bedroom, and looked over the trunk again. I'm glad this is mine. If Cleo wants it back, I'll give it to her. Regan went into the hall. Several people passed her on the way to the other rooms.

She went downstairs and out the door. Luckily there was still a good crowd of people. Not everyone had left in a huff. The girls were busy collecting money. One security guard was standing by the gate, checking people's bags as they were leaving. "You have to talk to Jody" was the response when people tried to haggle over prices.

Then she saw him. Mr. Invertebrate! He had a fish tank at his feet, and two goldfish bowls probably won years ago at an arcade on the boardwalk in his hands. He was waiting to pay. Kit should see this, Regan thought. She'd never let me hear the end of it. Regan started to turn away, hoping he wouldn't see her.

Too late.

"Regan?"

Here we go, Regan thought. She turned back to him. "Winston? Oh, hi." She walked over. "How are you?"

Winston stared down at her, a disapproving look on his face. He was tall and wiry, his sun-streaked hair falling onto his forehead. "I know you were trying to avoid me."

"No I wasn't."

"Yes you were, and your friend didn't like me."

Regan's mouth formed an O and she started shaking her head. "*No,* she liked you, Winston, I'm sure she did."

"If she liked me, she would have called me back. I left her three messages. It's okay. I'm over it."

"I think the problem was that she had been dating this other guy she liked but it didn't work out, and you know, she wasn't quite ready," Regan hastened to explain, then cleared her throat. "I see you found a few things you like," she said, changing the subject.

"Uh-huh. I'm off this week so of course I was at the beach. I saw the plane fly overhead announcing the sale. It was hot so I figured, why not? I wanted to get something of Cleo Paradise's to give to my sister but there's nothing left. Luckily, I found these," he said, holding up the fishbowls, "so it wasn't a wasted trip."

"Oh, great," Regan said with far too much enthusiasm. "It's a shame you didn't get anything of Cleo's but the people at the front of the line made a beeline for her stuff. Whoosh!" Regan laughed.

"My mother always said, the early bird catches the worm."

Are worms invertebrates? Regan wondered.

"My mother would be disappointed that I missed out on Cleo's things. So I'm not going to tell her I was here."

"Can I ask what you're doing here?" Winston said, his tone flat.

"Well, my mother was friends with the family when she was in high school, so we stopped by," Regan said, realizing that she'd given the same evasive answer a few minutes ago.

"Excuse me," one of the workers said to Winston. "Can I help you?"

"Yes, please," he answered. "Regan, your friend is very rude. Goodbye," he said, turning away abruptly.

"'Bye," Regan responded, a little surprised at her dismissal. I feel terrible, she thought as she turned away. It's so hard to set people up. Chances are it's not going to work out. She looked around. My mother and Edna must be in the back, she thought as two men approaching the front gate caught her eye. Neither one of them looked happy.

Instinctively Regan walked toward them. "I am Cleo Paradise's agent on record!" the older man was saying to the security guard. "I demand to see whoever rented this house to my client!"

34

Slowly but surely Cleo and Dirk inched up the trail. He tried not to lean on her too much.

"Are you sure you're okay?" he kept asking. "I don't want to hurt you."

"I'm fine. I really am."

When they finally reached Dirk's cabin he unzipped a pocket of his bathing suit, reached for his key, and unlocked the door. He hesitated for a moment, then made a decision. "This step is too high. If I lean on you too hard when I hop up, I could knock you over."

Cleo started to protest but Dirk wouldn't listen. He swung around, sat on the floor inside the door, and shimmied backward. He then pushed himself up as Cleo grabbed his arm to steady him.

Dirk's cabin was larger than Cleo's and more like a real home. The downstairs room was bigger, so was the kitchen. There was a small dining area and bedroom on the main floor. The loftlike bedroom looked exactly like Cleo's.

"You okay?" Cleo asked, guiding Dirk as he hobbled to one of two couches situated on opposite sides of the fireplace.

"I will be. With you helping me, how can't I?"

When he reached the couch, he sat down and let out a sigh of relief.

"Do you have an ice pack?"

"No. If you just wrap some ice in a plastic bag, that would do it."

Cleo walked over to the open kitchen. She was exhausted and knew she'd better drink some water soon. But first she wanted to get Dirk the ice. Quickly she opened drawers till she found a plastic bag. After she filled it, she grabbed a towel from the bathroom and hurried over to the couch. Dirk's foot was up on the coffee table. His head was back.

"I'm not much of a nurse," Cleo said.

Dirk leaned forward. "Thank you, Connie," he said as he put the towel under his foot and positioned the ice pack around his ankle.

"Would you like some water?"

"That would be wonderful. There's a big bottle in the refrigerator."

A minute later Cleo was back. She sat on the couch, handed Dirk a glass, then drained her own in one gulp.

Dirk smiled. "You were thirsty."

"I should have had water after my run. I think that's why I got stomach cramps."

Dirk leaned forward again and adjusted the bag. "I hope I didn't sprain it too bad," he said, groaning.

"Do you want to go to the hospital?" Cleo asked. "I'll drive you."

"No, not yet. If it gets really bad I'll go. I'm hoping my ankle will be okay if I keep this ice on there for a while."

Cleo was torn. She didn't feel comfortable staying with Dirk, but she also didn't want to desert him. She was afraid to be in her cabin, but the thought of packing up and finding someplace else to go was daunting.

Dirk's head was back and he looked like he was in pain. "I'll leave if you just want to close your eyes and relax," Cleo offered.

Dirk reached out and touched her hand. "No, please. Stay," he said, then closed his eyes.

"Okay," Cleo said. She put her glass on a coaster on the table. I'm so tired, she thought, as she leaned back and tried to relax. Maybe I'll close my eyes as well. For just a minute. Then something caught her eye that changed her mind.

The butt of a rifle was sticking out from under the couch.

35

I've been studying with the most wonderful teacher in Los Angeles," April informed her luncheon companion as the waiter cleared their plates. "Since I've been in his class I've experienced such growth as an actress. It's incredible. Even when I'm not doing a scene, I learn so much from his critiques of the other actors. I soak up every word he says, like a sponge." April's hands flew into the air, landing strategically on her chest, just above her low-cut blouse. She leaned forward. "You know what he told me after I did my very first scene?"

"What?"

"He told me I come to life when I act."

"Really."

"Really! Then after I did another scene he said he was amazed at my versatility. One scene was from a drama, the other a comedy. I love to do both!"

Sandy Stewart looked at his Rolex. The fiftysomething producer had a meeting in a half hour. Stewart had agreed to meet April Dockton for lunch as a favor to a friend of his in the business. She was certainly attractive, but much too desperate. "That's wonderful," he said, pulling his wallet out of his back pocket.

"This is my lunch," April said, putting her hand on his. "Before you leave, I insist you have dessert." She laughed. "I insist. They have yummy apple tarts topped with homemade cinnamon ice cream."

Sandy patted the side of his thinning blond hair. "I'm losing what I want to keep," he said, then pointed to his waist. "And gaining what I want to lose. No dessert, especially ice cream."

"They have noncaloric sorbet."

"No thanks. I really have to get going. I have a meeting."

"Is it about your movie?"

Sandy turned his head and gestured to the waiter. "Check?" he said, then turned back to April. "Yes, it is about the movie. We're meeting with the casting director to talk about actors we'd like to approach for the roles. Now that we have a decent script . . ."

"I hear it's a great script."

Sandy shrugged. "We hope."

The waiter approached with a small leather folder. Sandy whipped out a credit card and extended his arm before the waiter even reached the table. "Here. Thank you." he said.

"Honestly," April protested. "You were supposed to be my guest today."

Sandy shook his head. "I wish you a lot of luck in your career . . ."

Ever the actress, April kept smiling. "My teacher says we have to be pushy if we want to make it in this business," she joked. "I hear there's a fantastic part for someone my type in your movie."

"There is."

"Great," April responded, willing her laugh not to sound fake. "I'm ready to audition."

Sandy put his hand on April's. "Listen, honey. I understand

how tough it is. But it's tough for us, too. We want to make a movie that people will come see. A good script is important but it's vital for us to cast actors who have names. Actors who will bring people to the box office. If there were a smaller part for you, I would call you in. But there's not. Maybe next time."

The waiter returned with the credit card receipt. Sandy scrawled his name, picked up his card, and with a decisive motion, snapped the leather case closed. It reminded April of a judge with his gavel. Case dismissed.

"I understand," April said, trying to retain her dignity. "But someday you'll be begging me to be in one of your movies."

"That's the spirit."

"I have a question."

"What?" Sandy asked as he pushed his chair back.

"Who are you considering for the part?"

"We've tossed around a few names already. I probably shouldn't say . . ."

"Come on," April coaxed. I want to know—who's my competition?"

Sandy smiled broadly. "My personal favorite is Cleo Paradise." He reached out his hand. "It was lovely to meet you, April," he said, shaking her hand. "I've got to run. Let me know if you're in something I can see." He turned and hurried out of the restaurant.

36

Beaches along the Jersey Shore were mobbed. Ten miles south of Edna's house, in Seaside Heights, Rufus "Dizzy" Spells, his wife, Monique, and their three young sons trudged across the hot sand until they found a spot as close to the water as possible.

"Yippee," the youngest boy cheered, dropping his towel and kicking off his shoes. "I'm going swimming!"

"Me, too," his brothers both shouted, doing the same.

"Guys, what about suntan lotion?" Dizzy asked, resting a large beach umbrella on the sand.

"We put it on before we left the house," Monique said, chewing on a piece of her favorite hard candy. "You were in the car honking the horn."

"I wanted to get out of there," Dizzy grunted. "We planned to go to the beach at ten this morning. Naturally, that didn't happen." He started to twist the umbrella pole into the sand.

"Can I help you with that?" Monique asked halfheartedly. She put down her beach bag, took off her blouse, and adjusted the straps of her black bikini.

"Nah," he answered. "Watch the kids. Don't let them go in too far."

"I won't," she said, inspecting her tan line as she walked away.

With great effort, Dizzy pushed and twisted the pole down into the sand until he was satisfied it would stay upright. He let the pole go, his hand ready to catch it if it started to fall over. Happily the pole remained upright. Pleased at his accomplishment, he turned the crank and watched as the umbrella slowly spread out above him. A moment later he was arranging his towel, when the umbrella collapsed. A group of teenagers sitting nearby snickered. Dizzy didn't realize one of them had grabbed his cell phone and was videotaping the proceedings.

Dizzy stuck out his tongue and bit his lip. Concentrating hard, he grabbed the handle again, turning it until he heard the click that ensured the umbrella was locked in place. He plopped his body down, exhausted, and sighed with relief.

What a month, he thought as he unzipped the beach bag and fished around for the suntan lotion. Visiting Monique's parents at their beach house was usually fun, but this year her aunt and uncle were there, as well as her cousin who did nothing but complain. The house was too crowded and always noisy. Dizzy fumbled through Monique's comb and makeup and books and candies and bottles of water. Finally he spotted the lotion and reached for it. The bottle was hot and greasy and slipped through his hands. Give me a break, he fumed. Why can't Monique be more careful? He grabbed the bottle again, flicked the cap to the open position, aimed it at his thigh, and squeezed. To his amazement, the cap fell off. Runny lotion poured out of the bottle onto his leg, spilling over onto his towel.

The obnoxious kids laughed again, louder than ever. Dizzy ignored them. He threw the empty bottle in the sand, and leaned back on his elbow. His sons were splashing in the water, having the time of their lives. Like Monique, they were dark-haired and tanned easily. Not like Dizzy, whose pale skin got splotchy and red when he stood near a window. At least my boys are having fun, he thought. A lot more than I did at their age.

Thirty years ago, when Dizzy was in the first grade, his classmates had come up with his nickname. Rufus Spells became Dizzy Spells. Rufus told himself that he didn't mind. Dizzy sounded a lot cooler than Rufus. But the fact that Rufus was a bit klutzy ensured that the nickname stuck. He had always been good-natured about it, until Cleo Paradise decided to imitate him in that movie. He seethed at the thought. She'd turned his whole life into a joke. Now he wasn't only Dizzy, he was the "Dizzy Super Super."

She had some nerve imitating my walk, my mannerisms, the way I stick my tongue out when I'm hard at work. She was tiny but managed to master my clumsy gait. After the movie was released, everyone Dizzy knew realized she had used him for inspiration. After all, Dizzy was the superintendent of her building in Los Angeles.

I wish I'd never been nice to her. I went out of my way to help her out when she overflowed the bathtub, when her shade fell down, when she needed someone to hang a mirror, when the battery in her fire alarm started beeping and she had no idea how to change it. What does she do in return? She makes me look like a jerk. I'd told her about how wonderful the Jersey Shore is, and how my kids love to come visit their grandparents every summer. Next thing I know, she decides to rent a house at the Jersey Shore. What next, Cleo? he wondered. I'm sick of you. You used me and made my life miserable.

He lay back on his greasy towel and closed his eyes. The sounds of the surf, kids playing, even the lifeguard whistle, were soothing. Try and relax, he told himself. We'll be going home soon. I won't have to deal with Monique's relatives again until next summer.

He felt himself drifting off. He could hear the seagulls flying above. It was so peaceful . . .

"Dizzy!" Monique screamed.

Dizzy bolted upright. "What? What? Are the kids okay?" he asked as he got up from his towel, slipped, fell back down, then got up again. He ran toward her.

"Yes, but look!" Monique said breathlessly, her hair dripping. She pointed up at the sky. A plane was flying overhead, dragging a sign advertising a garage sale. A sale featuring Cleo Paradise's belongings. "Was Cleo Paradise at the Jersey Shore?" Monique asked Dizzy accusingly.

"I don't know," Dizzy lied.

"Are you sure?"

"Of course I'm sure. What are you, crazy?"

"It's obvious she likes you. She was always asking you to help her in her apartment. Dizzy, I need this. Dizzy, I need that. She couldn't change a lightbulb herself."

"Likes me? She made fun of me in that movie. Besides, she always gave me a good tip when I did things for her. You know that."

"I told you you spent too much time with her."

"No I didn't!"

"I think you secretly love the attention you're getting from that movie. You say you don't, but you do. It wasn't that bad. What she did was cute and funny."

"I don't love the attention!" Dizzy growled. "I'm sick of that kind of attention! I've had it my whole life and I'm sick of it!" His head was spinning. I really am dizzy, he thought. I can't stand

Cleo and my wife thinks I'm carrying on a secret affair with her. That woman has made my life miserable in yet another way.

Monique's dark eyes bore into his. "Every time you went out to get ice cream on this trip you were gone way too long."

Dizzy pointed at her. "That's because your relatives are driving me crazy. I needed some space! I wanted to eat my ice cream cone in peace. Can't you see how stressed out I am? Can't you?"

"You haven't been yourself this whole month. It's not fair to me. My relatives are good people. Good people, Dizzy. We see your nutty family in Los Angeles all the time."

"We see my family, but we don't live under the same roof with them. If your cousin knocks on the door one more time when I'm taking a shower . . ."

"I told you to take shorter showers. Every day we run out of hot water thanks to you."

Dizzy put his hands to his head. I can't take this anymore, he thought. This is all thanks to Cleo Paradise. "Maybe I'll just get out of your way," he said. "I won't use up any more of your family's hot water!" He turned on his heel and stormed back toward their spot.

The umbrella had fallen over.

Dizzy barely noticed. He grabbed his shoes and his shirt and kept going.

37

Hey, man, take it easy," the bulky security guard advised the two men at Edna's front gate. "Don't get excited . . ."

Regan approached them. Cleo's agent? she wondered. He hardly looks like the type who represents an Academy Award–nominated actress, with that ratty jacket and his scruffy hair. And that other guy doesn't look as if he'd be part of Cleo's world. "Did I hear you say you're Cleo Paradise's agent?" Regan asked.

The older man turned to her, his face indignant. "Yes, I am," he answered, throwing back his shoulders and straightening up. "My name is Ronald Flake, founder and president of the Flake Agency. Cleo Paradise would be nowhere without me."

"Got that right," his companion muttered. *"No-where."*

"This is my son, Horace," Ronald explained. "He accompanies me on all important business. Cleo hasn't returned my calls. She isn't hiding here, is she?"

Regan shook her head. "No."

"Are you the owner of the house?"

"No, I'm not."

"Is the owner here? I have some questions for her."

And I have some questions for you, Regan thought. "Mrs.

Frawley is around back," she informed them, introducing herself, but not mentioning her profession. "My mother is a friend of the family and is back there with her. Follow me."

"Very well," Ronald said, trying to sound like a visiting dignitary.

No one seemed to notice the hubbub surrounding the Flakes arrival. Zealous shoppers were too busy inspecting all the paraphernalia that was spread out on the lawn.

Ronald and Horace walked through the gate, nodding to the security guard, and started to follow Regan toward the side of the house.

"Dad, wait!" Horace ordered.

"What?" Ronald asked impatiently as he and Regan both stopped in their tracks.

Horace pointed. "Look at those rubber mats. And a cup holder. I could use a few things for my car—"

"Not now!" his father snapped.

Poor Cleo, Regan thought. These two are her front men? No wonder she's not returning their calls.

They continued around the side of the house. Straight back was the garage, to the right the pool house. They walked toward Nora and Edna, who were sitting in the gazebo overlooking the pool.

"The first time I saw *The Sound of Music,* I told my husband I had to have a gazebo," Edna was saying to Nora. "We went out and bought one the next day."

"I remember that story," Nora said politely.

Edna giggled. "What Karen probably never told you is that she used to come out here and dance around and sing that 'Sixteen Going on Seventeen' song. You know the one that I mean?"

Karen would kill you if she heard this, Nora thought as she nodded. "Of course! It was a great scene in the movie. The oldest Von Trapp daughter and her boyfriend are singing to each other in the gazebo, then it starts to rain . . ."

"Exactly! Karen was so cute, dancing and singing, wishing that one day she'd have a boyfriend who would sing to her like that, who wanted to take care of her." Edna then rolled her eyes. "So who's the first boy she brings back here? A kid named Fish. Suited his personality. Believe me, there was no singing. Oh, here comes Regan . . ."

Edna stood as Regan approached, followed by two men who were lagging behind. They don't look so suave, Edna thought, but it's always nice to have male company.

Ronnie Flake eyed the sparkling blue pool, a beach ball floating whimsically on its surface. His jaw tightened as he took in the lush greenery, the brightly colored flowers, the beautiful backyard that would look better when all the junk and shoppers were cleared out.

"Cleo could never have afforded to stay here if it weren't for you, Pops," Horace whispered. "She didn't have two nickels to rub together when you met her."

"I know it. Your mother and I didn't go on vacation this year to save a few dollars. She would have liked coming down here for the day." He shook his head. "She would have liked to sit in that outside thing like those two ladies, and have her beer."

"That's a gazebo," Horace informed him.

"Who do we have here?" Edna called as the two men walked around the diving board.

"Let me introduce the Flakes," Regan said. "Ronald and his son, Horace. Ronald is Cleo's agent."

"You're Cleo's agent?" Edna repeated, as she shook his hand. Was he here to collect Cleo's things? she wondered nervously. Too late. Her stuff is all gone.

"Yes, I am her agent. I must have a talk with you."

"Please have a seat," Edna said. "Make yourselves comfortable. Would you like water?" she asked, indicating the pitcher and glasses on a little wicker table in front of her. "It's such a hot day."

"No beverage. This is business," Ronald answered, trying to sound important.

Nora looked at Regan. "If this is private . . ."

"No!" Edna said. "Stay. Everyone sit down."

Edna's protest and the look on Regan's face froze Nora in place.

Whew, Regan thought as she sat next to Horace, whose short-sleeved nylon shirt was sweat stained under the arms. His moccasins were worn out, his cheap white pants sporting what looked like a fresh coffee stain. No wonder he wanted that cup holder, she thought.

"Where is Cleo Paradise?" Ronald blurted, his tone rude.

Edna's hospitable expression disappeared in an instant. "How should I know?" she answered haughtily.

"She rented your house, didn't she?" Horace demanded, as though that were a good enough reason for Edna to keep track of Cleo's whereabouts.

"Yes, she did, and she left."

"You say she left to do a movie?" Horace asked accusingly.

"I didn't *say* anything," Edna answered. "Cleo left a note stating she was off to do a movie. That's all I know."

Horace stood and stepped toward her. "Listen, lady," he said, pointing his finger threateningly. "You know and you're not telling us. Cleo hasn't answered my father's calls. She can't sign a contract for another movie without him! Tell us where she went!"

Regan stood and moved toward him. "Horace, you'd better—"

Horace swung around, bumping into the table. "I'd better what?" he demanded as the pitcher and glasses crashed to the floor.

Edna screamed and lifted up her feet.

"You'd better get out of here!" Regan shouted into his face as the security guard manning the back lawn came running over, quickly followed by the guard from the front gate. They grabbed the Flakes by their necks and, despite the father's and son's loud protests, escorted them off the premises.

The three women followed.

"Well," Edna said breathlessly as she and Regan and Nora watched the Flakes get thrown out the front gate. "At least I got my money's worth out of those guards. They're such nice fellows, aren't they?"

38

In the office at the Log Cabin resort, Gordy was feeling a little bummed. Bummed and jealous. He had found Miss Long's bathing suit, brought it up to her cabin, and hung it on the line when she didn't answer the door. And Dirk wouldn't let him take any credit. I should have left a note, he thought. Now she'll never know what I did for her. If I tell her I'll get in trouble. But what did she think when she saw it there on the line? Wasn't she surprised?

Right now she and Dirk are splashing around the lake together, Gordy thought. I wish I'd paid more attention to her when she checked in last Saturday morning. It was so early and I was tired and talking on the phone. Then one of the groundskeepers had taken her in the golf cart up to her cabin and that's the last I saw of her. To the best of Gordy's knowledge, Miss Long had hardly emerged since. Except of course when I try and do a good deed and hope to see her. It's then she's out for a jog.

Gordy had peeked out the window when Dirk and Miss Long headed across the parking lot together. She sure was cute. And closer to my age than Dirk's, Gordy thought. She can't be more than twenty-two or twenty-three. I'm seventeen and Dirk is already thirty-two. He's too old for her! Gordy had worked at the resort all summer. It didn't seem like his boss dated much, but he sure seems to have taken a shine to Miss Long.

I could kick myself, Gordy thought. When I went up there this morning, she didn't open the door because she wasn't dressed, but she sounded so sweet. Then I had to joke that it reminded me of when my mother had curlers in her hair and didn't want to be seen. How dumb was that! She must think I'm a complete nerd.

Sighing, Gordy looked up at the clock. He realized that it was almost time to leave. On Thursday afternoons, he volunteered at a day camp for underprivileged kids. The camp had a special program where teenaged volunteers like Gordy showed up once a week, played baseball with the boys and girls, had dinner with them, followed by a campfire where they all sang and told stories. Everyone went home by nine. Thursday was the only late night at the camp and the kids loved it. Sometimes Gordy would bring his computer and give lessons on how to use search engines for schoolwork. Gordy willingly admitted he was a techno geek. His mother always teased him about it. *Gordy,* she'd say, *when I was growing up we had one phone—a landline—and no call-waiting or caller ID. If Aunt Jessie sat on the phone all night, blabbing with her boyfriend, no one could get through. We didn't have computers, or cell phones . . . It was a different world.*

It must have been horrible, Gordy thought. If there was a new gadget on the market, he would buy it the day it came out. With his own hard-earned money.

I've really got to go soon, Gordy realized. But Dirk wasn't back yet and Gordy always talked to him before he left for the day. Dirk was funny like that. If you left without saying good-bye, he'd get insulted.

"Mrs. Briggs?" Gordy called out to the woman who worked in the back office paying the bills and organizing the paperwork.

"Yes, Gordy," she answered.

"I have to go soon. It's Thursday."

"I know that, dear."

"Dirk isn't back yet. I don't know if I should leave."

"Why don't you give him a call?"

"He's down swimming."

"I know that, dear. But if he's not actually in the lake, he'll answer his cell phone."

"Okay." Gordy picked up the phone and dialed his boss.

Dirk answered after two rings.

"Dirk?"

"Yes, Gordy."

"It's time for me to leave. I just wanted to let you know."

"Okay, Gordy, that's fine. I had a little mishap."

"What?" Gordy asked quickly.

"I think I sprained my ankle. Miss Long helped me back to my cabin."

"You and Miss Long are at your cabin?" Gordy asked, his voice cracking, then regretted his reaction.

"Yes. Miss Long prepared an ice pack for me. If my ankle doesn't feel better soon, she'll take me to the hospital."

"Oh gosh," Gordy said. "I hope it's not sprained. You'll have to be on crutches . . ." Secretly he was pleased. No more swim dates for his boss and Miss Long.

"It's okay. I can get around the camp with the little cart. We'll see. Tell Mrs. Briggs I'm here if she needs me."

"I will. See you tomorrow."

Gordy hung up the phone. Miss Long is taking care of Dirk! How unfair! Gordy picked up his backpack, informed Mrs. Briggs of Dirk's malady, then went out to the parking lot.

I found her bathing suit this morning, he thought as he walked to his car, I returned it, and now she's taking care of

Dirk. Miss Long's car was right there next to his. Gordy stared at the big SUV as he got the keys out of his pocket. She's such a little thing, driving a big car like that. All the way from California. Does her front tire look a little low? he wondered. He crouched down on the ground to take a look. It was fine. Too bad. Then he glanced under the car hoping to find something else of hers. If he did, this time he wouldn't leave it on any clothesline. He'd give it to her in person.

But there was nothing. Just grass. He was about to get up when he spotted something under the bumper. Gordy looked closer. It was a GPS tracking device, he was sure of it! Does Miss Long know it's there? She might, some people have them in case their car is stolen. Or did a jealous boyfriend secretly install it? Gordy wondered. If so, Dirk better be careful.

Gordy stood, unlocked his car, and got in. Should I tell her? he wondered as he backed out. No. If she knows it's there, then she'll wonder what I was doing snooping under her car. She drove a long way to get here. Maybe her family wanted her to have the tracking device for safety so they'd be able to find her if they didn't hear from her. That must be it. She's so sweet. I'm sure they worry about her.

Besides, Dirk would be mad if I interfered.

Pulling out of the parking lot, Gordy sighed. I let her slip through my fingers.

39

Cleo was about to make a mad dash for the front door of Dirk's cabin when his cell phone rang. He opened his eyes and grabbed the phone. *What am I going to do?* Cleo wondered nervously as Dirk spoke to Gordy. *Just because he has a rifle doesn't make him a psychopathic killer. He might have it for self-defense. But a rifle? When he finishes his conversation, I'm going to tell him I have to go back and work on the book I'm supposedly writing about meditation. Right now I could really use some secrets on achieving inner peace. I'm a nervous wreck.*

Cleo tried to keep her eyes away from the floor where the rifle was peeking out from under the couch. *I've got other worries,* she realized. *Like how did my bathing suit end up on the clothesline? Did someone follow me here? Are they hiding in the woods right now, waiting for an opportune moment to do me in?* Cleo's heart started pounding in her chest. *I'll go back to my cabin, pack up my things, and get out of here. I won't stop until I get to New York City where I'll check into a crowded hotel. Safety in numbers,* she thought. *I don't want to be alone.*

Finally, Dirk hung up his cell phone and tossed it back on the coffee table. "Gordy's leaving for the day," he said to Cleo.

"He's a good kid. I just have to keep after him sometimes. He is so young."

"He's very nice," Cleo said, then stood. "I should get going."

A slightly hurt expression crossed Dirk's face. "Why?"

"I have to go back and get some work done. Of course, I can give you a lift to the hospital first if you'd like . . ."

"Nah," Dirk said, leaning forward and adjusting the ice pack again. "You can wait hours in those emergency rooms. If it gets worse, I'll find somebody to give me a ride later." He looked up at her. "How does your head feel?"

"Fine," Cleo answered quickly. "I am absolutely fine."

"You sure you don't want to stay a while? We could listen to music, or watch TV, just relax."

"No thank you. Really."

Dirk frowned. "You changed your mind so quickly. I don't understand why, but it's your choice." Somewhat forlorn, he shook his head, folded his hands, then looked down at the ground.

"Okay. Let me know if you need anything," Cleo said as she made a beeline for the door.

"Ohhhhhh! Miss Connie! I know why you're leaving!"

No you don't, Cleo thought as she quickly reached for the door handle.

"This isn't a real rifle! I swear it isn't."

Cleo froze.

"I'm throwing it over to the other couch. Look at it, Connie, please. The last thing I want is for you to be worried that . . ."

Cleo turned her head as the rifle landed on the other couch, its barrel pointed in her direction. Dirk's eyes were twinkling. "I worked at a ranch out West for a while. When I was moving back home, my friends had that made for me for a joke. Look, it's a fake. It's got my name on it and the word "Ponderosa" because they knew I loved *Bonanza*. You ever see that show?"

Cleo nodded. "In reruns."

Dirk howled. "Of course in reruns! I saw it in reruns, too. We're both too young to have seen the original shows."

Cleo laughed in spite of herself.

"I keep the rifle under the couch because people come in here and get scared when they first see it. Like you did."

"No I didn't."

Dirk's cell phone rang again. He looked at the caller ID. "It's my mother," he said, then answered. "Hello, Mom . . . Mrs. Briggs got the news to you already huh?" Dirk winked at Cleo. "I'm fine . . . Yes, really . . . As a matter of fact, I've got a real cute girl taking care of me . . . Oh, you know that, too? . . . She almost left, 'cause she saw that rifle the boys from the ranch gave me sticking out from under the couch . . . I know I should put it away . . . Sure, here, talk to her." Grinning, Dirk held out the phone to Cleo. "My mother would like to say hello."

"Oh," Cleo said, clearly taken aback. She took the phone. "Hello, this is Connie."

"Connie, don't let my boy scare you. I told him to get rid of that stupid toy of his . . . How does his ankle look?"

"It's definitely swollen."

"Oh dear. Well, thank you for taking care of him."

"You're welcome," Cleo said. "Hopefully the ice pack will help the swelling . . . I'm sure he'll call you if it doesn't . . . Okay, then, it's nice talking to you . . . Bye now." Cleo handed the phone back to Dirk, shaking her head with amusement.

"Okay, Mom, I'll be fine. You and Mrs. Briggs have some hotline going . . . Yes, I'll let you know if it gets worse . . . I promise . . . Talk to you later . . . Love you, too." Dirk snapped his phone shut, threw it on the table, and smiled at Cleo. "We have a close family." He rolled his eyes. "As you can see, not much that I do gets by my mother. But it's great. My parents live about an hour from here so I see them a fair amount."

Cleo smiled. "You're lucky. My parents travel all over the world so I don't get to see them much."

"Do you have brothers and sisters?"

"No."

"That must be hard to have no family around," Dirk said softly.

"It's lonely sometimes." Cleo shrugged her shoulders.

"Well, sometimes I get lonely even when I'm with my family. But I guess you're used to spending time alone. You must like it," Dirk said teasingly. "You've barely come out of your cabin all week."

Cleo made a face. "I told you I have work to do."

"Connie?"

"Yes."

"You're very mysterious."

"Why? Just because I'm working hard?" Cleo asked, enjoying the playful exchange. "Some people call that discipline."

Dirk looked into her eyes. "You're an intriguing little lady. A very cute one, too."

"Well, shucks," Cleo joked.

"I don't know about you, but I'm kind of hungry."

"Me, too," Cleo said.

"You mind fixing us some lunch? I've got plenty of food in the fridge."

Cleo smiled. "Sure. Why not?"

Dirk laughed and slapped his thigh. "You *were* scared of me!"

"No I wasn't!" Cleo protested dramatically as she headed toward the kitchen. "You don't scare me!" she said, laughing. "Not in the least!" With you I feel safe, she thought. Other things scare me, but I'm putting them out of my mind right now.

She started to poke through the refrigerator.

Dirk called from the couch. "What's taking so long?"

Cleo laughed. "Oh, be quiet!" That does it, she thought happily. I'm living for the moment. I can't be so afraid anymore.

If only she'd waited one more day to change her thinking . . .

40

Here goes, Scott thought as he pulled up to the security booth at the gated community of the couple he and Jillian had met the night before.

The guard opened the window. "Can I help you?" he asked, in a somewhat hostile tone.

"Hello," Scott said cheerily, then gave his name. "I'm here to meet with the Binders."

"They're expecting you." The guard pushed a button and the gate started to open. "Make a right and follow the road. After you pass Oakley Way, it's a few houses down on the left."

"Thank you, sir," Scott said, continuing his cheery act. It's showtime. When an event was about to start, that's what Hayley would say to her workers. It's showtime, everybody! Scott pulled through the open gate. I hope everything works out so I can see her on Saturday, he thought. We always have a good time.

The houses in the complex were all attractive one-story brick structures, built very close together, obviously well cared for. There wasn't a single one that screamed for the attention of a handyman. Not like the neighborhood I spent my early years in, Scott thought. One neighbor's front yard was nothing but overgrown weeds, another guy painted his house a neon color that made Scott wince, then let it peel, and a third idiot never bothered to remove a plastic display of Santa and his reindeer from the roof when the Christmas season was over. A windstorm the following July blew it onto the front lawn, where it remained for months.

Scott located the Binders' home, parked in front on the narrow, curving street, and turned off the car. Everything was so calm and orderly, he felt a little nervous. This might not be so easy. People who were too orderly weren't his best targets. He preferred the type whose paperwork was in a jumble and who couldn't keep track of their affairs. With resolve, Scott grabbed his briefcase, got out of the car, and walked up the path to the front porch. He pointed his well-manicured finger at the buzzer and pressed hard.

"Scott!" Betty Binder exclaimed when the door flew open. "How lovely to see you again." The tiny eighty-six-year-old woman was dressed in pale pink pants, a short-sleeved pale pink top, and white sneakers. Her white hair was well coiffed, her pretty, lined face carefully made up just like last night. She grabbed Scott's hand. "Come in, dear!"

"Thank you." He stepped into the beautifully appointed foyer and glanced around. "This is lovely."

"It's home," Betty chirped, obviously pleased. "I love to decorate. Isn't that stone tile pretty?"

"Gorgeous," Scott answered, then looked in her eyes. "I have to tell you. It was such a wonderful surprise to meet you last night. I can't get over it."

"For us, too!" Betty grabbed Scott's arm as she gazed up at him. "I get chills thinking about that moment when Jillian screamed, 'Yes! Yes, I'll marry you!' I love romantic movies but to witness a beautiful moment like that in real life . . ." She put her hands up to her face. "I get all teary-eyed thinking about it.

And then to have the chance to spend time with you and Jillian, such nice young people. It just doesn't happen very often in this crazy world."

Scott put his arm around Betty and tenderly patted her frail shoulder. He could almost feel her swoon, hoping she got a whiff of his expensive cologne. "I'm so lucky," he said, willing his voice to crack. "I'm more than lucky, I'm blessed. Jillian means the world to me. I can only pray we have as long and happy a marriage as you and your husband."

"You will," Betty said, clutching Scott's elegant suit jacket. "I know you will. Come, please." She took his hand.

Scott followed Betty down the hallway into the tastefully furnished, spotless living room. Nothing was out of place. A small, walled-off backyard, resplendent with colorful flowers and plants, was visible through sliding glass doors. Bright patio furniture and a state-of-the-art grill set the scene for summer entertaining. This is all bad for me, Scott thought. Their lives are too orderly.

White-haired Ed Binder emerged from a hallway, moving slowly. He was wearing khaki pants, a red short-sleeved shirt, and like his wife, a pair of white sneakers.

"Hello." His gravelly voice greeted Scott.

"Hello there, Mr. Binder," Scott replied, extending his hand. "I was just saying to Mrs. Binder that I hope Jillian and I have as many wonderful years together as—"

"Scott, I told you last night," Betty interrupted with mock exasperation. "Call us Betty and Ed."

Scott laughed. "Okay. I will." He shook Ed's hand, then turned. His gaze fell onto a framed black-and-white wedding photo obviously taken many moons ago. "Is this . . . ?" he asked, raising an eyebrow and walking toward a table full of pictures.

Betty beamed. "Yes, it's us. Sixty-seven years ago. What a day. It was so rainy."

"You looked beautiful," Scott said.

"She still looks beautiful," Ed muttered.

"She certainly does."

"Enough, you two," Betty joked, her face glowing. "Let's sit. Scott, I fixed a special lunch. I hope you'll break bread with us after we talk business."

"I don't want you to go to any trouble . . ."

"No trouble at all."

"Thank you. That would be an honor." Scott's eyes quickly scanned the photos on the table. There was one other wedding shot. "I have to ask," he said, "who's the lovely bride here?"

"Our daughter. Diane is our only child."

"She's beautiful, too."

"Thank you. Diane was married thirty years ago. She and her husband, Brad, moved into a tiny studio apartment in New York City. Now they're so rich you can't believe it!"

Scott laughed. "Really?"

Betty rolled her eyes. "Brad got involved in the television business and then the Internet business. They have two huge homes and are always on the run. He's a little quiet for my taste, you know, the strong, silent type, but he's been a good provider. And Diane's happy. She hasn't changed a bit. She tries to buy us things all the time but we won't let her. We take care of ourselves. Right, honey?"

Ed nodded. "I never asked anybody for anything." He took a monogrammed handkerchief out of his pocket. "Never will, either."

"She sounds like an amazing person," Scott said. "But how could she not be? She had two loving parents who gave her a good home, everything she needed, and raised her with the right values. Not every child is that lucky. That's why I started a charity that helps children all over the world. Now Jillian will be working with me. She's already been involved, of course. But now it's official."

"A charity for children?" Betty asked, her eyes widening. "How marvelous. I want to hear all about it. Scott, can I get you anything to drink?"

"No thanks, I'll wait until lunch. It's so great to see you two again," he said as he sat in a chair opposite the couch where Betty and Ed were settling in.

"Scott, what's your charity called?" Betty asked quickly.

A saintly expression came over Scott's face. "Most Precious Treasures."

Betty's hands flew to her mouth. "I'm going to cry."

Ed nodded. "Good name. Children are our most precious treasures."

"What exactly is it your charity does?" Betty asked.

Scott leaned forward. "I've got to tell you. It's the most rewarding thing I've ever done in my life. Our board has quarterly meetings to decide where to distribute our money, which children in need will receive our aid. It's always a tough, tough meeting. We get so many requests. Right now there's a school in South America that was practically destroyed by a flood. They're rebuilding and are in desperate need of supplies. We're sending a check out next week. It's not enough to cover everything, but we do what we can." Scott leaned over, picked up his briefcase, and opened it. "When I'm feeling down I look at these photos for inspiration. It motivates me to keep going, keep working." He took out a manila envelope and handed it to Betty. "These are pictures of children we've helped all over the world."

Scott passed the photos to Betty and Ed. "Look at their faces," Betty said. "They're adorable! Why, they're precious!"

Scott smiled as Betty handed him back the envelope. "They certainly are precious," he repeated, his voice husky. He then removed another envelope from his briefcase. "And these are pictures of some of the celebrities who have contributed to Most Precious Treasures." He handed Betty the second envelope.

"Oh, you're in all these pictures!" Betty said with delight as she rifled through the photos. "Ed, look at all these stars posing with Scott!"

"I'm looking."

"Those stars are good people," Scott said solemnly. "They often get criticized for being too Hollywood or too self-absorbed. But let me tell you, when it comes down to the basics, they're just like you and me. They care about the future of our children."

"Oh, Scott!" Betty exclaimed. "This was all meant to be. Ed, to think we almost decided to stay in last night and cook hot dogs."

"We came pretty close. I was starting to heat up the grill and you decided you wanted chicken with snow peas."

"Meant to be?" Scott asked innocently.

"This morning Ed and I had a long talk about money. We knew we'd be discussing financial planning with you and possible investments, but do you know what we ended up talking about?"

"What?" Scott asked, trying to remain calm.

"Making a difference in people's lives. We have plenty of money to live on. Our grandchildren have big trust funds and don't need our dollars, which on the one hand is great, but on the other makes us feel, well . . ."

"Like you're not as needed as you'd like to be?" Scott suggested helpfully.

"Yes!" Betty said. "That's exactly it. We're thrilled that Diane and Brad have so much. But we've never been able to experience the joy of giving our grandchildren something that their parents couldn't afford. They already have everything! Just today we decided we'd give more of our money to charity, and list more charities in our wills. But we didn't know where to start. And here you are, telling us about a charity that helps children. That's perfect for us! Children who need us! I'm telling you, there are no coincidences!"

"None!" Scott agreed.

Two hours later, Scott drove away with a check made out to Most Precious Treasures. A check for fifty thousand dollars.

More was promised.

41

Edna," Regan began. "The person who called before—"

"Look!" Edna cried joyously, pointing across the street. "My friends from Golden Peaks!" She dashed off to greet them.

Four elderly women were waiting out of harm's way until the Flakes were good and gone.

Nora looked at Regan, a half smile on her face. "Karen told me she was glad Edna had hired security guards. Wait until she hears how hard they had to work. But everything else seems okay around here. You know, Regan, it's Edna's right to sell her house. Look how happy she is with her new friends. She's excited about this next phase of her life."

"Mom?"

"Yes."

"Everything's not okay."

"Regan, what do you mean?" Nora asked quickly. They were standing on the side of the lawn, talking quietly. Shoppers were milling all around.

"Didn't you think there was something odd about Cleo Paradise leaving behind those skulls?" Regan asked. "She's an actress with a high profile. Why would she leave herself open to criticism about her strange taste?"

"I did think it odd, but who knows? Some actors would want the publicity. I just saw a picture of an actress happily walking her goat down the street in Los Angeles. I kid you not. No pun intended. And how about the actor who sleeps with his pet pig?"

Regan shook her head. "I understand, but I don't think that's what Cleo wanted. The phone call I answered for Edna? It was Cleo's best friend . . ."

Nora's face grew concerned as Regan told her about the conversation with Daisy. "Someone left dead flowers in this yard while Cleo was staying here?"

Regan nodded. "Yes, and that's what a stalker did in Cleo's last movie. The movie was a bomb. Cleo didn't think it was serious enough to report. She must have been scared but she didn't leave. Something else must have happened that drove her away."

"You're right, Regan. But you said Daisy spoke to her Monday night, and she just left her a message in the last hour. Cleo could be fine. Daisy's going to call you if she hears from her?"

"Yes," Regan answered. "Maybe Cleo just wanted to hide out. She's obviously avoiding that agent and I don't blame her for that. But if she were doing a movie, she would have told her best friend. The whole thing doesn't feel right."

"No, I guess it doesn't."

"And remember the blonde we met at the front gate?"

"Yes. She was very sweet."

"She's Scott Thompson's fiancée."

"What? The one you saw last night?" Nora asked excitedly, trying to keep her voice down.

"The very one. She didn't show any sign that she recognized me. No reason she would. Her back was to me in the restaurant and she did get engaged, so her mind was on other things. I guess the ring didn't fit—she's not wearing it. Poor Hayley."

Jody popped her head out the front door. "Mrs. Frawley!"

"Yes, Jody," Edna yelled, waving her arms. She was proudly leading her friends onto the property.

"There's a phone call for you. It's important."

"Who is it?"

"Just come in, please," Jody ordered, then went back inside.

"Excuse me, ladies," Edna said. "I'll be right back."

Regan and Nora looked at each other, then followed Edna up the steps into the house.

"Who is it?" Edna asked Jody, who was waiting in the vestibule.

"I didn't want to shout so everyone would hear," Jody said quietly, her hand covering the mouthpiece of the wireless phone. "It's Cleo Paradise's mother."

"Oh my!" Edna exclaimed, feeling a slight pang of guilt. She thought of how Karen wanted to make sure no one went anywhere near her things with a ten-foot pole. Did Cleo Paradise's mother get wind of the sale? She might be upset for her daughter. "Regan," Edna whispered. "Would you be a dear and talk to her for me? If it's really important, let me know." She dashed back outside without waiting for a response.

Regan took the receiver from Jody, then motioned to Nora to follow her. Earlier, Regan noticed a laundry room off the kitchen where they could have privacy. "Hello."

"Edna Frawley?" a woman asked. She sounded far away.

God no! Regan thought. "Actually, I'm a friend of Mrs. Frawley's. She's tied up at the moment. My name is Regan Reilly. May I help you?" She and Nora reached the laundry room and stepped inside. Regan closed the door and turned the receiver outward so Nora could lean in and listen to the conversation.

"This is Yaya Paradise. I'm Cleo's mother. Her father and I are on holiday in Ukraine. The woman who answered the phone told me Cleo isn't there. She was quite abrupt and said she was running an estate sale."

"That woman is running a sale for Mrs. Frawley today," Regan explained, remembering reading that Cleo's parents traveled around the world. "She *is* busy, but I'm sorry if she seemed rude. As for your daughter, Cleo moved out of here last week."

"Last week? I thought she was extending her stay until her friend Daisy could meet up with her," Yaya said anxiously. "Where did she go?"

"She left a note saying she was off to do a movie."

"Why wouldn't she tell us in an e-mail? Or call us with that kind of news? I couldn't reach Cleo on her cell phone. I'll try and get in touch with Daisy. They were planning to drive back to California together . . ."

I have to tell her, Regan thought. If Daisy tells her that she also spoke to me, Mrs. Paradise will think I'm trying to cover up something. And I'm concerned myself. "Mrs. Paradise," Regan said, "Daisy called a little while ago. She doesn't know where Cleo is, either."

"What?" Yaya asked, clearly alarmed. "Daisy doesn't know where Cleo is?"

"Apparently not. But they just spoke Monday night." Regan then explained to Yaya that Daisy was concerned because Cleo didn't tell her about any film or that she'd moved out. Hesitantly, Regan told Yaya about Cleo's belongings being sold at the garage sale. May as well, Regan thought. It's on the Internet.

"What did Cleo leave behind?" Yaya asked, her voice sharp.

"She left clothes in the washer and dryer, some odds and ends, and a collection of skulls . . ."

"Our skulls?" Yaya screamed.

"They're your skulls?"

"Yes! Cleo's father and I sent them in a trunk to the house. Cleo was going to bring them back to our storage unit in California. For years we've collected artifacts from around the world. Our dream is to open a museum. Cleo knows how much every item we collect means to us. She would never have willingly left that trunk behind! Never!" Yaya started to cry. "Cleo said in an e-mail that Frawley woman could be exasperating. She's worse! She couldn't wait to have her little sale and make a dime off my daughter. What happened to my Cleo?"

"I understand how upset you must be," Regan said.

Cliff was standing close to Yaya, listening to the conversation, just as Nora was with Regan. He grabbed the phone.

"This is Cleo's father. She said she left to do a movie? Maybe we should call that crazy agent of hers."

"He was just here," Regan said. "He doesn't know where she is, either."

"Call the police!" Yaya screamed.

"I'm a private investigator," Regan said. "Cleo wouldn't be classified as a missing person yet. You and Daisy both just tried Cleo's cell phone in the last few hours. It's not as if she hasn't returned calls for days. You haven't been waiting long to hear back from her."

"I don't care if it's been five minutes or five days. Something's wrong!" Yaya insisted. "I just know it. It's not like Cleo to go off and not tell anyone. We'll get back to the States as fast as we can. Please look for our daughter! Please find her! We'll pay you whatever you want. It won't be a wild-goose chase, I promise you!"

"Let me get your information," Regan said as Nora dug a piece of paper and a pen out of her purse. Leaning on the washing machine, Regan took down the Paradises' worldwide cell number and Cleo's cell phone number and address. "What about her car?" Regan asked. "Do you have the make and model or possibly the license plate number?"

"Oh no, we don't! It's one of those big SUV type of things. She just got it to drive cross-country." Yaya sounded on the verge of hysteria.

"Don't worry, I'll ask Mrs. Frawley," Regan said. "Maybe she has some of that information. Please try not to get too upset. There could be a simple explanation. Hopefully you'll hear from Cleo very soon."

Yaya whimpered. "Call us when you hear anything. We're on our way."

When Regan hung up the phone, she and Nora were silent for a moment. "And I didn't even tell them about the dead flowers," Regan said.

"What are you going to do?"

"I don't want to make phone calls from here. I'll go out to the car."

They walked out of the laundry room. Regan replaced the receiver in the kitchen while Nora went to find Edna. In the living room, Jody had just completed a sale. "Pull up your truck to the front," she said to an older woman accompanied by two muscular young men. "Then come in and get the couch."

"Jody?" Regan asked after the threesome were out of earshot.

"Yes," Jody answered, giving the clear impression she didn't want to waste time talking.

"Cleo's parents sent her that trunk with the skulls from Europe because they're planning to open a museum. They're sure Cleo didn't mean to leave it behind. Is there any way we'd be able to get the skulls back from that couple and refund them the money?"

Jody tried to smile. "Oh, Regan. You saw how crazy those two were. Did they really look to you like they would ever give back anything associated with Cleo Paradise?"

42

On the 747 headed from San Diego to Newark, Karen Fulton was restless. After sitting on the tarmac for what seemed like forever, they'd finally taken off. She was checking her watch every two seconds. A watched pot never boils, she thought. But a watched watch is even worse.

She sighed. When I think of all the days I don't have enough time. I rush around but still can't get everything done. And here I am stuck in a middle seat for another four hours with nothing to do but worry. My computer is dead, I've already seen the movie they're showing and didn't like it, and the book I was reading is inside my bag that's crammed into the overhead bin. I didn't have time to dig it out when I boarded the plane and I don't dare try and retrieve it now. Maybe when the movie is over I'll get up my courage. But the flight attendants already can't stand me.

I probably should have called Frankie and told him what's going on, she thought. But it's so hard to reach him on the cruise ship. He's in and out of his room, and the time difference between us is always changing. Not that he'll care about the house being sold. He's been away for so long. But once the house is gone, things will never be the same. Tears welled in Karen's eyes. It's where Daddy breathed his last. All those memories. My boys got up on surfboards for the first time at the Jersey shore.

Karen's twins, now in their twenties, lived in San Diego and were trying to find themselves. You should look someplace besides the beach, Grandma Edna had told them more than once. They'd gotten such a kick out of Cleo Paradise renting the house and were hoping to meet her one day. Too late now, Karen thought. Something tells me the last thing Cleo Paradise will ever want is to have anything to do with our family.

I'll get out my sleeping mask, Karen decided, as she reached underneath the seat in front of her for her purse. Not that I'll sleep, but maybe I'll relax. I hate these day flights. Better to get on a flight in the evening, have a cocktail, and nod off.

A moment later Karen pulled the elastic band of the mask over her head, arranged the pale blue protective covering around her eyes, and leaned back. Immediately she felt a tap on her shoulder.

"Excuse me, Miss," the man next to her said. "Before you fall asleep, I'd better go to the bathroom."

"Sure," Karen said, trying to sound patient, as she pulled down her mask.

"You look like you're heading to a Halloween party."

Karen smiled. "No, actually I'm going to a garage sale," she said, her tone wry.

"That's a long trip for a garage sale," he said as they both started to get up. "But my wife loves them. Years ago, she bought a painting that was worth so much more than what she paid for it. Since then, she can't pass a garage sale without slamming on the brakes. That painting was a steal!" He smacked the top of the seat in front of him. "A real steal! And she's found tons of steals ever since!"

43

Outside Redman's, Hayley and Laurinda were air kissing good-bye.

"Mmmmwa," Laurinda said as their cheeks brushed. "Thanks for lunch, Hayley. Mmmmwa."

The producer who had been dining with April Dockton came out the door and rushed past them.

"Oh," Laurinda said. "I want to get out of here before April emerges. Talk soon." She turned and hurried down the block to the theater.

Hayley stood for a moment on the sidewalk. She'd had to push the thought of Scott to the back of her mind and act like a professional who was at the top of her game while she was with Laurinda. Now, left alone, her thoughts returned full force to her own problems. A sick feeling came over her.

Turning on her heel, she started toward Broadway. Even though the air was hot and sticky, she felt the need to walk a few blocks before she found a cab. Images of Scott came rushing back to her. He got engaged last night, then asks me out Saturday? What is going on? Will his fiancée be out of town?

I have to call Regan and tell her. Hayley reached in her purse for her BlackBerry. She checked her e-mails and saw that her assistant had sent several messages that were marked as urgent.

Hayley dialed her office. "Angie, what's going on?"

"Super news, Hayley! A big television producer from L.A. just got to town. He wants to create a buzz for a new reality show he's doing about celebrity therapists and heard what a great party you organized last night. He'd like to meet with you right away."

"Define 'right away.' "

"He's sitting by the pool on the rooftop of his hotel in SoHo. Isn't that cool? Can you join him now?"

"Of course." Hayley walked to the curb and hailed a cab. Better to focus on work, she thought. I'll call Regan after my meeting.

While the cab rattled downtown, Hayley searched her Black-Berry for all the background information she could find on her prospective client. When she stepped onto the rooftop of his hotel, the producer was easy to spot. Deeply tanned, he was sipping champagne and surrounded by half a dozen young assistants.

"Hayley, darling, is that you?" the producer asked, raising his designer sunglasses.

Here we go. "Yes, it is," Hayley said with a big smile. "I am so thrilled that you called. . . ."

44

*C*leo Paradise is a goner.
I wish I didn't have to wait until tonight.

45

━━━◆━━━

Regan started out to her mother's car, then decided to talk to Edna first. It wouldn't be easy to hold her attention for too long with everything going on, but Regan had a few quick questions. She found the self-described garage sale hostess in the backyard, standing near the pool with her friends. Edna was introducing Nora while one of the security guards swept up the broken glass inside the gazebo.

"And this is Nora's daughter, Regan," Edna beamed. "Say hello, Regan."

"Hello, everyone. Edna, could I speak to you a moment? It's about the phone call."

"Certainly. Excuse me, ladies. As soon as that gentleman is finished, we'll have lemonade in the gazebo."

Regan led Edna to a corner of the backyard. "Edna, Cleo's mother is very concerned. So is Cleo's best friend, who called earlier. They don't know where Cleo went."

"Neither does that creepy agent," Edna pointed out, her eyes blinking repeatedly. "Wasn't he the worst? And that son of his? If I were Mr. Flake, I'd keep him under wraps."

"They were a pair," Regan agreed. "Edna, please think for a

minute. Is there anything Cleo said to you that might give an indication of where she may have gone?"

"Honestly, Regan, there isn't. Clearly she wanted to be left in peace and quiet. Privacy was paramount to her." Edna shrugged. "She didn't welcome my overtures of hospitality. I was living nearby and told her if she needed anything to please call. The only time I heard from her was last week when she called and asked if it might be possible to extend her stay for a week or so if need be. I told her that would be fine, just let me know. Then I never heard back. I left messages over the weekend, but nothing. Then I came home Sunday, the day she was originally supposed to leave, and found the note. It would have been nice if she called, one way or the other."

"Do you have any idea how she spent her time when she was here?"

Edna shook her head. "Not really. But I heard she'd gone into town and talked to people. This was after she made me promise not to tell anyone that she was here. I know word got around. I had to tell my maid to take the month off. With pay, I might add. But the young man who takes care of my pool had to come by twice a week. He also cuts the grass and tends to the flowers. That has to be done regularly. The inside of your house can hide a lot of sins, but not the outside. Before I left I told him a young lady would be renting the house for the month of July. But my lips were sealed as to her identity."

"Have you spoken to him at all lately?"

"No, he doesn't call unless there's a problem. His bills always arrive in a jiffy, I'll tell you that much."

"So you don't know if he ever actually met Cleo?"

"No."

"Can I have his number?"

"Of course. I have it memorized. He's been with me for several years now."

Regan copied the number down on the piece of paper she'd used to write Cleo's information.

"Judson mows the lawn every Friday. The sound his mower makes could wake the dead. What a racket. But he's got a green thumb and is a hard worker. As you can see"—Edna pointed around her yard—"he does a lovely job."

"He does," Regan agreed. "Thanks, Edna. One more question. What kind of car did Cleo drive?"

"It was white, one of those big SUV-type cars. I noticed it had California plates."

Edna touched Regan's arm, her expression suddenly serious. "Cleo is probably okay, right?"

"Probably," Regan said, trying to appear optimistic. She turned and walked through the yard, then down the block to her mother's car. I'm glad we found a spot in the shade, she thought as she unlocked the door. When she got inside, she turned on the engine and the air conditioning. The last thing I need is for anyone to overhear me, she thought.

First I'll call Hayley. I'm almost afraid to tell her Scott's fiancée was here. But Hayley's voice mail came on.

"Hayley, it's Regan. Please call me." Hanging up, Regan sighed. Hayley didn't give me her office number. She hadn't told anyone she'd hired a private investigator to trail Scott and didn't want to speak to Regan from her office.

Next Regan placed a call to Judson. His voice mail picked up as well. She left a message.

When she called Jack, she was grateful he answered the phone.

"Hey there."

"Hi," Regan answered. "Finally someone wants to talk to me."

Jack laughed. "How's the garage sale? Did you buy me a present?"

"Wait till you hear this," she said.

Jack's eyes crinkled as he listened and concentrated on what Regan was telling him.

"Cleo's parents are really upset. So is her best friend. But I have to be careful. Cleo's a high-profile person. She might have gone off with some guy and doesn't want people to know."

"I understand. You want some help?"

"What?"

"I got called to a meeting in Newark so I stopped at the apartment first and picked up our bags. My meeting just ended. I'm on my way."

Regan smiled. "That's the first piece of good news I've had all day."

46

Scott's heart was racing with excitement. New York City, here I come, he thought. I've got to deposit the Binders' check in my account before they change their mind. Now I can pay off that loan. Jillian would kill me if she knew about it. I've got to stay away from those gambling tables in Atlantic City.

I'll deposit the check, then turn the car around and get back across the bridge before rush hour. He'd made plans to go to the house his grandfather had owned in a rural area of western New Jersey. As a kid, Scott enjoyed visiting his grandparents at their big, old house and playing in the barn out back. Grandpa had died last year and the family was fixing up the place before they put it on the market. Because his grandfather had never wanted to move out, and was running out of money in his later years, he'd taken out a second mortgage on the property. By the time it sold and the family paid the taxes, there'd be nothing left. He tried to call Jillian but she didn't pick up. She must be tied up at that other garage sale, he thought.

He looked down. I'm going to need gas soon, he realized. I certainly rack up the mileage on this car.

His cell phone rang. It was Trevor.

"Trev, how are you doing?"

"I'm bored, Dad. I can't believe I've been stuck up here since July Fourth weekend with nothing to do!"

"Sorry, Trevor. But it was your mother's decision to vacation in Maine, away from all your friends. Where is she?"

"Out on the beach with the old guy."

Scott smiled. No love lost there, he thought. Good. "I really wish you could be here right now, Trev, I really do. We'll have to wait until next Friday. Then we have two weeks together."

"No, Dad, get this. Mom is sick of listening to me complain. She said I could fly down tomorrow. Isn't that great? After you pick me up at the airport, maybe we could take my friends to dinner. I'll call the guys. On Saturday there's a Yankee game . . ."

Scott's stomach dropped. "Oh, Trev, I don't know . . ."

"What, Dad? You don't want me to come down early?" Trevor asked, both hurt and incredulous. "You just said you wished I could be there right now!"

"I do! But this weekend I'll be out at Grandpa's house. We still haven't sold it. I've arranged to have workers come and do more repairs. It never ends!" he said, trying to laugh. "Why don't you get a flight on Monday night or Tuesday? We'll—Trev?"

His son had hung up.

Scott redialed but Trevor didn't answer. No sense trying to make up more excuses, Scott thought. I'll make it up to him next week.

If I get the chance.

47

Horace was speeding toward the Garden State Parkway.

"What's wrong with you?" Ronnie asked, as he pounded the dashboard. "Look what you did! My reputation is ruined. All the years of hard work in this business and it comes to this. I can't show my face anymore."

"Me?" Horace screamed. "You weren't exactly polite to that woman."

"I didn't point my finger at her in a threatening way! Maybe I was coming across a little tough at first, but it was all part of the dance. I knew what I was doing! Ronald Flake has successfully negotiated many a contract, after all."

They were about to pass a train station. Abruptly Horace turned the wheel to the left, sped into the parking lot, and screeched to a halt.

"What are you doing?" Ronnie cried.

"Get out!"

"Get out? Are you out of your mind?"

"No, I'm not. You can't yell at me like that!" Horace shouted. "Get out of my car. The train is coming. If you hurry, you might get a good seat."

Ronnie looked at him aghast.

"Get out!" The blood vessels in Horace's forehead looked as if they might pop.

Quickly Ronnie obeyed, but then slammed the door with all his might. It was barely closed when Horace took off.

Such a temper, Ronnie thought. Wait till his mother hears this.

48

In the ladies' room at Redman's, April stared into the mirror. As soon as Cleo Paradise's name had been mentioned, her blood had started to boil. And boil and boil and boil. It showed on her face, which was so red it almost matched the color of her hair. *I'm only twenty-seven but I look so old*, she thought. *All this stress! If I don't get a great role soon, I may as well be put out to pasture.*

Cleo Paradise. Why couldn't she have continued wandering the world with her vagabond parents? The cutesy little story that weirdo Yaya told in all the interviews about three-year-old Cleo doing a dead-on imitation of someone they met in the wilds made April want to throw up. *She's such a mimic. So talented. The way she disappears into a character is amazing. She can play any role at all!*

April quickly touched up her makeup. Tomorrow she was heading back to Los Angeles. She'd been back and forth between New York and Florida a few times in the past month and had been so excited to finally nail down this lunch date. *What a disaster! I'm so mortified*, she thought. *Mortified.*

On the way out of the restaurant, she did her best to act like a star.

"I'll be back soon, I promise," April cooed, hugging the maître d'.

Out on the street, the marquee sign for *The Tides Return* made her wince. Before lunch it hadn't really bothered her. Now it seemed like another slap in the face. I'm surprised they didn't want Cleo for that part, she thought angrily.

She hailed a cab.

"Where to, lady?"

"The rental car place straight down by the river."

49

After Regan hung up with Jack, she felt so much better. He'd be with her in the next hour or two. Now I'll try Cleo, she thought. She probably wouldn't pick up if she didn't recognize the number, but I'll leave a message.

Regan dialed, then waited as Cleo's cell phone rang several times. Finally the voice mail kicked in, but it wasn't Cleo's voice. An automated recording gave the number called, and said to leave a message after the tone.

"Hello, Cleo, my name is Regan Reilly. I know this call is coming out of the blue and you might be inclined to ignore it, but if you would call me back, I'd appreciate it. I'm at Edna Frawley's home. Your parents and friend Daisy have called here because they haven't been able to reach you and are very concerned. Your parents are on their way back to the States and Daisy's on a movie set, so if you call them and end up having to leave a message, I won't know you're okay until someone gets back to me. I'm a private investigator and your parents want me to locate you as soon as possible. Please call and let me know you're okay. Thanks, Cleo . . ." Regan gave her number then hung up.

Regan sat still for a moment, thinking. When she hears I

know Edna, she may never want to talk to me. I hope the guy who takes care of Edna's pool gets in touch soon. He must have run into Cleo at least once during the month.

Regan's phone rang. She looked at the caller ID and smiled. It was Kit. "What's going on?"

"Nothing," Kit answered. "I'm sitting outside on my lunch break and I thought I'd say hello. I also wanted the latest update on that guy you were spying on. Your client's love life sounds worse than mine. Anything new?"

"As a matter of fact . . . ," Regan began. Then she described the scene at the Chinese restaurant. But Regan never named names.

"He's engaged!" Kit exclaimed as she watched a pigeon peck at a crumb perilously close to her sandaled feet.

"There's more." Regan told her where she was and why. "The fiancée is working at this garage sale."

"Oh my God!" Kit cried. "Does your client know yet?"

"I tried to call her but she didn't pick up. It can wait."

"If I were her, or she, or whatever is the proper word, I'd want you to find out every detail about that other woman. Every last detail! And that woman might be interested to know that lover boy was seeing someone else as recently as last week."

"Last week? He wanted to go to a big party with my client last *night,* but she couldn't bring a date. So he gets engaged. He probably would have sooner or later, but still."

"I hope your client doesn't go the route of, 'Oh, if only I brought him to the party, that would have been the night he fell in love with me.' "

"No, I don't think so, Kit. She's out for blood."

"Good."

"And I have some other interesting news for you," Regan said, a smirk on her face.

"What?"

"Guess who I ran into at this garage sale?"

"I'm stumped."

"Winston."

"Mr. Jellyfish?!" Kit almost shrieked. "What was he doing at a garage sale?"

"Snapping up two goldfish bowls and a fish tank."

"Oh my God! Reilly, you will never ever ever have a career as a matchmaker."

"How did I know that would be your reaction?"

"Because I'm so predictable. Okay, I can understand why he purchased those hot items, but why was he at the garage sale in the first place?"

"He saw a sign that said some of Cleo Paradise's things would be for sale and wanted to get something of Cleo's for his sister. But all of Cleo's stuff was already gone when he got here. By the way, he told me you never called him back but he was over it."

"What a relief. Maybe he met someone else."

"Maybe," Regan said. "But he didn't look exactly thrilled."

"He didn't look thrilled on our date."

"Kit, I'd better get going. There's something more serious going on . . ." Briefly Regan explained her new case involving Cleo Paradise.

"Hopefully she wanted to try someplace new while she waited for her friend," Kit said.

"Hopefully," Regan agreed. "But her parents have enough reason to be worried."

50

"How about an omelet?" Cleo called to Dirk. "I'll cut up a green pepper and a tomato and throw in some cheese."

"That sounds great."

"What would you like to drink?"

"You mind making a pot of coffee?"

"Not at all."

Fifteen minutes later Cleo carried a tray with their lunch into the living room. She placed it on the coffee table and sat down.

"Here you go." She handed Dirk a plate with a steaming omelet and a toasted English muffin. "And here's a fork and napkin."

Dirk smiled. "This looks wonderful."

"You'd better taste it first before you comment."

"You didn't mix any poison in there, did you?"

"No," Cleo said matter-of-factly. "The bottle was empty."

They both chuckled and dug into their food.

"This is delicious," Dirk said after he took a bite. "Really good."

"It does taste pretty good, if I do say so myself."

Dirk winked at her. "I could get used to this."

"Being waited on?" Cleo teased.

"Being waited on by you."

Cleo took a sip of her coffee. They ate in silence, neither one having realized how hungry they were.

When Dirk was finished, he patted his mouth with his napkin and leaned back. "That hit the spot. Connie, you're a good cook."

"Thank you."

"I'd like to know more about you."

"What do you want to know?" Cleo asked lightly.

"You live in California, right?"

"Yes, Los Angeles."

"And you're writing a book on meditation. How did that come about?"

Cleo hated to lie. But she didn't want to tell Dirk who she was yet. She didn't want her fame to get in the way. It was nice to just enjoy each other's company.

"Well, I figured meditation was a good way to calm my *noives*. My *noives* were shot."

Dirk at first was startled, then cracked up. "Really? Your noives?"

Cleo's eyes twinkled. The performer in her was coming to the surface. And if I'm going to try and deflect the conversation away from my life, I may as well have fun, she thought. "Yes. Absolutely. They were shot! Which reminds me of the joke about . . ."

Dirk listened, his face incredulous, as an animated Cleo told three jokes in a row, using different accents and voices. It was her delivery that was so funny. He was laughing even before she got to the punch lines. "I never would have guessed there was a side like this to you, Connie," he said finally, wiping his eyes, chuckling, and shaking his head. "Whew. You were so quiet and so serious . . . You really do . . . ," he started to say, then couldn't get out the words. He'd obviously thought of something funny and started to laugh again.

"I what?" Cleo asked.

". . . you do need meditation!" He pointed to the door and guffawed. "You better get back to your cabin right now and write that book!"

Cleo burst out laughing. "Well hardy har har," she said as she started to clear the plates.

"No, don't do that now," Dirk said, waving his hand at her to stop.

"I thought you liked being waited on."

"I do. But I want to hear more jokes. When I laugh I forget about the pain in my ankle."

"Poor baby."

"I am a poor baby."

"You just said I should go write my book," Cleo teased. "Good idea." She started to get up.

"No!"

"I really should go change out of my bathing suit."

"No you shouldn't," Dirk insisted. He reached for her hand. "I'm not letting you go."

51

Jillian was doing her best to remain cheerful, even though Striker and Harriet were not happy people. When Jillian had gone into the house, Harriet had cried out, "How could you have made me throw out the flowers Striker sent me our first Valentine's Day together?"

"And my mementos," Striker said angrily. "The program from the first Bruce Springsteen concert I ever went to. Tossed in the trash."

"They were in a box in the attic gathering dust," Jillian said sweetly. "Harriet, you told me yourself you never looked at them."

"But we knew they were there!"

"I planned to go through that stuff eventually and use it for inspiration to write songs," Striker said, running his hands through his hair. He threw his head back in despair. "Faded photographs," he yelled, "tickets torn in half, remember that song? People collect those things!"

"We didn't throw out any photographs," Jillian said, in an effort to console him.

"I'm making a point!"

"Sorry," Jillian said. "Let's have the sale and I promise you'll feel better."

"Where is the trash?" Striker asked. "Harriet said you took it with you."

"I learned from experience that's it's always better to get rid of the stuff people agree to part with as soon as possible. There have been times when I've helped people clean out their clutter, then come back for a second day of hard work, and what do I find? Their junk is back! They fished through the garbage in the middle of the night. But you know what?"

"What?"

"I convince them to throw everything out again," Jillian said with a knowing smile, "and they end up being so grateful. I promise you will, too. Striker, you don't need a dusty box of mementos to inspire you. You're a brilliant musician."

Striker shrugged and looked down.

"It's true." She made a fist and pumped the air. "Let's move on and have a great sale!"

Grudgingly, Harriet and Striker helped Jillian display their things on the lawn. But people didn't flock to the sale. One young mother came by and started to browse through the items baking in the sun. Her five-year-old kept tugging at her arm. "It's too hot, Mommy. I want to go swimming."

"Okay! We'll leave."

A couple came and bought a dresser and an old desk. Another woman bought a few pieces of jewelry.

"Well, that's a relief," Harriet said. "This hasn't been a total waste."

"Oh yes it has," Striker said, staring at Jillian. "It's been more than a waste."

52

Dizzy drove and drove, his thoughts frenzied. It was bad enough having his friends mock him when that stupid movie came out, but Monique had always been on his side.

"I love you, Dizz," she'd say. "Don't pay attention to any of those people who are making fun of you. They're just jealous." Now for Monique to suggest he had a thing for Cleo was outrageous! If Monique knew how he really felt about Cleo, she'd be scared.

He vividly remembered when Cleo moved in. Sure, he didn't mind that she was beautiful and friendly. Who needs another grouchy tenant in the building who did nothing but complain? Since she had just come from New York, Cleo didn't have any furniture. Just a couple of suitcases. A bed she'd ordered was delivered that first day. Within a couple weeks, she'd bought a couch and chair and end tables and lamps. If he spotted her carrying boxes or groceries from her car, he'd run and help. She was fun, easy on the eyes, and nice to his kids. And then she used him.

Monique's going to be furious that I left her at the beach with no car, he thought. Too bad. She can call that annoying cousin of hers for a ride home. I'm not going back until I'm good and ready.

And that won't be for a while.

53

Regan found the landscaper's address on her BlackBerry, then got out of her mother's car and walked back down the block to Edna's home. Nora was sitting in the gazebo with Edna and the women from Golden Peaks.

"Wilbur has such a crush on you," one of the women was saying to Edna. "It's so obvious. I think he's fallen in love!"

Edna beamed. "We do enjoy each other's company. I'm so lucky I sold this house! I can't wait to live at Golden Peaks!"

"Here's Regan," Nora said.

Regan waved as she approached the gazebo. "Hello, everyone. Mom, I'd like to take a ride into town. I shouldn't be gone long."

"Go ahead," Edna answered before Nora could open her mouth. "Nora, stay with us. Regan said she'll be right back."

"Sure," Nora answered, shrugging her shoulders slightly.

Regan returned to the car and was heading down the main street of Edna's quaint little town when her cell phone rang. Oh good, she thought when she looked at the caller ID. It was the landscaper. She put in her earpiece and answered. "Hello."

"Hello, I'm returning your call. This is Judson."

"Judson, thanks for getting back to me," Regan said, then

explained the reason she wanted to speak with him. "I just left Mrs. Frawley's and was planning to stop by your office and see if you might be there."

"No, I just finished a job and am heading into Sam's Deli to grab a sandwich. It's right on Main Street. You want to meet me there? They have tables in the back. I can't stay too long. I have another lawn to cut today."

"Sounds good."

A few minutes later, Regan walked into the deli. At the last table, Judson was wolfing down his sandwich. He looked to be in his late twenties, tanned and muscular, with dark hair cut close to his head. He was wearing jeans, a T-shirt with grass stains, and work boots, and started to stand as he greeted her.

"Please sit. Thanks for meeting with me," Regan said as she pulled out the chair opposite him and sat down.

"Sure. What's happening?"

"As you know, I'd like to speak to you about Edna Frawley's former tenant."

He smiled as he took a sip of his bottled iced tea. "Cleo Paradise?"

"You knew who she was?" Regan asked.

"Everybody in town knew. Come on. This is a small place. Gossip around here goes viral." He grinned. "I know she's gone now. Why are you asking about her?"

"Her parents are concerned because they haven't heard from her this week. They called the house while I was there. They're parents so of course they worry," Regan said. "They asked me to try and find out where Cleo is. She's probably fine, but I was wondering if you had much of a chance to talk with her at all."

"The first few times I went over to cut the lawn or check the pool her car was there but she stayed inside the house. Then I went over and found her in the pool doing laps. She got out right away so I could do what I needed to do. She was really nice and introduced herself as Cleo."

"She did?" Regan asked, surprised.

"Yes, but she only gave me her first name. We chatted while I skimmed the pool and added the chemicals. I was cool," he said, nodding his head. "I didn't let on that I knew who she was, even though I was dying to tell her I loved that movie where she played the super. They dyed her hair red and cut it short for that movie. Now she has shoulder length brown hair, so I guess she's not too surprised if people don't act like they recognize her."

"I got the impression from Edna she wanted her privacy. She got a lot of mean press after her stalker movie."

"Yes, but come on. She must have gotten lonely. She told me a friend was supposed to be with her for the month but couldn't make it. After that she'd sit out and chat whenever I worked on the pool. I obviously can't have a conversation when I'm mowing the lawn."

"Right," Regan said.

"Since she didn't tell me her last name, I didn't want to make her uncomfortable by asking about her movies. Then last Friday I was cutting the lawn when a delivery truck pulled up. They unloaded a big box for 'Cleo Paradise c/o Edna Frawley.' She wasn't home so I put it in the garage in case it rained before she got back. That box was a mess! The cardboard was all beaten up and ripped, so I pulled it off. The next time I saw her I was going to tell her that I'd put her trunk in the garage and wow, you're Cleo Paradise, the actress."

"The trunk was delivered last Friday?" Regan asked.

"Definitely. I cut Mrs. Frawley's lawn every Friday."

"Cleo left for good Friday night but didn't bring the trunk

with her. Did you leave her a note saying it had been delivered and was in the garage?"

"Huh?" Judson looked embarrassed. "Oh, man, no, I didn't. But she had to have known it was hers, right? I thought I was being nice getting rid of all that dirty packaging. Besides, the day before she had told me she probably was staying an extra week. I was sure I'd see her, and I was looking forward to it because I wanted to talk to her about the movie. Then I hear she's gone!"

"She told you on Thursday that she planned to stay?"

"Yes."

Regan frowned. "Do you know if Cleo parked her car in the garage?"

Sheepishly, Judson answered. "She didn't. She joked that she was sure she'd scratch the car if she did and the car was a brand-new Lexus SUV."

"So there's a good chance Cleo didn't even see the trunk before she left," Regan suggested mildly.

"Why do you keep asking about the trunk? When you find her, can't she come back and get it?"

"Mrs. Frawley is having a garage sale today. Everything that was in the trunk has already been sold."

Judson laughed out loud. "That doesn't surprise me. Mrs. Frawley is a piece of work."

Regan smiled and raised her eyebrows. "Judson, the trunk is not what I'm concerned about. I need to locate Cleo. Is there anything she said to you that might give a clue where she might have gone? Anything she talked about that you remember?"

Judson sat back and squinted his eyes. "Let me think. Well, she wouldn't go to the ocean again."

"Why not?"

"She said she liked the pool better because she'd been knocked over by a wave the first week she got here. It had scared her a lot."

"That can be really scary," Regan said. "So she wouldn't necessarily head for a beach area again. I'm just wondering where she'd go if she wanted to spend a few days by herself while she was waiting for her friend to join her. Someplace where she could relax."

Judson shook his head. "I don't know. I can't think of anything she said that might help."

"Thanks, Judson," Regan said, then gave him her number. "If you do think of something, would you give me a call?"

"Sure." An hour later, Judson was pushing his lawn mower across a large stretch of property. He was going over in his mind the moments he spent with Cleo Paradise. The last time he saw her she'd been reading a book by the pool when he arrived. I asked Cleo if she liked the book and she said she loved it. It was about a pioneer family living in a log cabin. She said she envied their simple life, he remembered. Should I call Regan Reilly and tell her that? Or would I seem really stupid?

Judson noticed a small rock in his path. He stopped, went around the lawn mower, and tossed the rock aside. He could tell Old Man Appleton was staring out the window, watching his every move. If I make a call right now, he'll start yelling.

Maybe when I finish this job I'll call Regan Reilly.

But he still wasn't sure.

54

Frankie went through the motions of his usual banter with the audience during cocktail hour but his heart wasn't in it. All he could think about was how he had completely blown the opportunity to buy the house from his mother. Couldn't she have at least called and given me one last shot when she got the offer? It would have been nice. But no, she goes right ahead and sells the family home without discussing it with me or Karen and is already selling everything out from under us. The worst part, Frankie thought, as his fingers glided effortlessly across the keyboard, will be telling Rhonda.

He hated to think that it was partially his fault. He never imagined he would want to go back to that house. But meeting Rhonda had changed everything. She was so right for him in every way. The fact that she lived at the Jersey Shore and had a restaurant where he could perform were added bonuses. Everything would have fallen perfectly into place if not for his mother. Now he would have to scramble to find a decent place for his new family to live.

When the cocktail hour was over, Frankie went back to his room and put a call through to Rhonda at the restaurant. One of her employees answered the phone.

"Is Rhonda there?" Frankie asked.

"Who's calling?"

"Frankie."

"Hold, please."

As Frankie waited, his body tensed.

"Frankie!" Rhonda said happily. She'd gone into her office and shut the door. "I didn't expect to hear from you until later."

"Hey, Rhonda," Frankie said, his tone glum. "There's something I have to tell you and I didn't want to wait. I'm afraid you're going to be disappointed, and believe me, I'll understand if you never want to speak to me again."

Rhonda's heart sank. She'd already told all her friends and half of Asbury Park about her engagement. "Frankie, if you've changed your mind about us, just say so."

"Changed my mind? No! Rhonda, it's nothing like that," Frankie exclaimed, his head starting to pound. "Oh my God, no."

Tears of relief stung Rhonda's eyes. Quickly she blinked them away. "Then what could possibly be wrong?" she asked.

"I called my mother. She sold the house a few days ago and is having a garage sale as we speak. I'll have to find another place for us to live, which probably won't be as big or have a swimming pool . . ."

"You think that would disappoint me so much that I wouldn't speak to you again," Rhonda asked incredulously, "never mind marry you?"

Frankie felt embarrassed. "Well, maybe . . ."

"Frankie, you want to know how I really feel about it?"

"Of course."

"I'm thrilled!"

"You're thrilled?"

"Yes! I already had one mother-in-law who didn't think I could do anything right. If we moved into the house and I started making changes, it would be a problem whenever your mother visited. You said she's opinionated, right?"

"That's putting it kindly." Frankie smiled broadly as he fell back onto his bed. "I love you, Rhonda."

"I love you, too, Frankie. We'll find a place here in Asbury Park and have fun fixing it up. This town is making a comeback. Artists and musicians who've moved here come into the restaurant all the time. We'll get a place for less than the price of your mother's house and it will only go up in value."

"How did I get so lucky to meet you?" Frankie asked, rubbing his forehead.

"You're blessed. We both are. You say your mother is having a garage sale right now? Should I go check it out?" Rhonda asked.

"No! I'm begging you. Stay away!"

"Frankie, I'm only kidding."

"Good. I don't want anything to ruin our plans. Like having you meet my mother when I'm not there. Rhonda, I really wish I could get off the ship tomorrow and catch a flight home," he said softly. "I miss you so much."

"I miss you, too. Two more weeks and you'll be here. I can't wait."

"Two more weeks," Frankie said. "Then we'll look together for a new place where we'll start our life fresh. I can't believe what a dumb idea it was for me to want to bring you and the boys to live at my mother's. It would always have seemed like her house. That wouldn't have been right." There was a knock at Frankie's door. "Just a second," he called. "Rhonda, I'd better get back to the lounge. I'll call you later."

Frankie hung up the phone and hurried to open the door. He was taken aback to find the cruise director standing in the hallway.

"Hello, Gregory," Frankie said. "What's up?"

"As you know, my nephew is making great sacrifices to take over your job so quickly."

Give me a break, Frankie thought, but kept his expression neutral. "I certainly appreciate that."

"He'll be coming on board tomorrow."

"Tomorrow?"

"Yes. That's what works best for him. He'll need to move into your room."

"My room?"

"Yes, Frankie, I'm sure you understand. The travel office will arrange a flight for you back to the States. You'll need to clear everything out before we dock in the morning." Gregory looked at his watch. "Don't be late getting back to the lounge." He turned on his heel and walked briskly down the hall.

Frankie fumed as he shut the door. You just had to stick it to me, didn't you? If I had asked if I could leave tomorrow you would have said no. Well, I'm thrilled, buddy! Just like Rhonda was a few minutes ago when I thought I was giving her bad news. He laughed. Should I call her back?

Yes, but I'll have to wait 'til later.

55

When Regan returned to Edna's house, the ladies from Golden Peaks, Gladys, Tilda, Dot, and Margaret were in full gossip mode with Edna. They barely noticed as she sat down next to Nora in the gazebo. I'll stay for just a few minutes, Regan thought.

"My daughter is arriving tonight," Edna announced. "I'll bring her over tomorrow to Golden Peaks and show her the unit I plan to buy. She'll be happy when she sees it. It will put her mind to rest."

"Will she be happy to meet Wilbur?" Dot asked, then covered her mouth as she giggled.

"She'd better be," Edna answered. "Who wouldn't be happy that Wilbur and I have found each other? Except, of course, that grouch Stix."

The ladies laughed.

"He's not happy at all," Gladys agreed. "It's ridiculous how jealous he is of the time Wilbur spends with you. Sunday night when he heard you were selling this house and planned to buy at Golden Peaks, he ran out of the pool room."

"Wilbur is such a nice man," Tilda said. "I don't know why

he bothers with Stix. And that nickname came from hanging around pool halls all his life. Is that something to be proud of? I should say not!"

Edna shook her head. "When I left Golden Peaks last Sunday I was so down. I knew I'd see Wilbur again, but I was afraid he might lose interest; you know—out of sight, out of mind, especially if Stix had anything to do with it. Then when I got the offer on the house I couldn't believe it! I was free to buy a place at Golden Peaks. Now, by hook or by crook, I'll seal the deal with Wilbur!"

The ladies shrieked with laughter.

"Stix has Wilbur to himself today," Edna said. "But not for too many tomorrows."

"I was surprised Stix wasn't playing in the pool tournament this morning," Dot said, looking from one to the other. "Where did he and Wilbur go?"

"Atlantic City."

"Atlantic City?" the three women said at once, their eyebrows raised. "Hmmm."

Edna shrugged. "Stix wanted to go down for the day and play craps. Wilbur is such a good egg. He understands that Stix isn't happy about my impending permanent arrival at Golden Peaks and he's trying to show Stix he'll always be his friend. What I don't understand is why Stix isn't interested in the companionship of a woman. Wasn't he married all those years?"

"If you think he's a grouch, I heard his wife was even worse!" Dot exclaimed. "She was a real shrew. No hankies were needed when she kicked the bucket."

"Dot!" Tilda protested as they all chuckled.

"It's true. At her funeral there wasn't a wet eye in the house," Dot proclaimed. "Stix's wife ruined him for the ladies. But who'd want him? Not me."

MOBBED

———◆———

"I guess it'll be a fight to the finish for Wilbur," Edna said. "Something tells me I'm going to win."

"You go, girl," Gladys said. "All is fair in love and war."

Jody had approached and was standing in the doorway. "Excuse me, Mrs. Frawley. A gentleman wants to buy the sideboard in the dining room. I told him it's not for sale but he's desperate to make an offer."

"My daughter would kill me!" Edna exclaimed. "It's been in the family for so many years." She stood. "Let's find out how much money he's talking."

"I'll be inside waiting for you," Jody said.

Nora looked at Regan as the whole group stood.

"Edna, we'll get going while you negotiate," Dot joked as the women filed out of the gazebo. "You've got a lot of deals going these days."

Nora and Regan pulled Edna aside as the others walked ahead. "If you promised Karen that sideboard, do you think it's a good idea to sell it? She's already upset," Nora said quietly.

Edna waved her hand, then whispered. "Don't worry. I'm not going to sell it. But maybe I'll talk the guy into something else," she whispered. "Jody said he's desperate. Come inside and watch me do my stuff," she said with a wink, then hurried to say good-bye to her friends.

Nora turned to Regan. "What happened in town?"

"I spoke to the landscaper about Cleo but he has no idea where she might have gone. I'm trying to figure out what to do next. In some ways my hands are tied. I can't put a trace on her cell phone or credit cards yet. It's too soon to call the police."

"Nora, Regan, come on."

They caught up to Edna and followed her into the house.

"Mrs. Frawley," Jody said, "this man just loves your sideboard and insists he's not leaving without it."

"Can I help you two with anything?" Jody asked the Reillys as Edna went into the dining room with the shopper.

"No, thanks," Regan answered.

"You two have been here for quite a while," Jody said, her smile forced.

Jody doesn't want us around, Regan thought.

"I'm sorry, sir, but I couldn't possibly sell that piece," Edna said, her voice loud and clear. "I'm not interested."

"Oh, Mrs. Frawley, why not?"

Regan turned to her mother and smiled. "Let's go watch."

Jody extended her arm to block the way. "Don't go in there, please."

"Why not?"

"If Edna decides to sell, she'll get a better price if no one is listening," she whispered.

Regan frowned. "You heard her. She doesn't want to sell the piece."

"She says that, but for the right price she might change her mind."

"She won't change her mind," Nora said decisively. "Let us through."

56

Daisy was trying hard to lose herself in the scene they were shooting which was supposed to be zany and fun. She and her new love pull to the side of the road to fix their flat tire and realize the engine isn't in the best shape, either.

What if Cleo's car broke down somewhere? Daisy wondered as the cameras were rolling. What if she decided to start driving down to Florida to surprise me? It's my fault if something happened to her. I already feel so guilty that she had to go to New Jersey all by herself.

After they did the first take, the director walked over to her, put his hand on her shoulder, and led her off to the side. "Daisy, I want you to look like you're having the time of your life. You and Kyle are madly in love and everything is wonderful. The audience has to feel that and fall in love with you, too. That way when April tries to strangle you they'll be jumping out of their seats and screaming. Capiche?"

"Capiche," Daisy answered. Cleo would be furious with me if I blew this scene worrying about her, she thought. She was always a pro. Like the time she was on her way to the set of *My Super Super* and someone sideswiped her car. Cleo was a little banged up but refused to go to the hospital.

"I can't be late," she'd told the police officer, and then asked him to call her a cab. Cleo said she'd done her best work that day. "I had to focus," she said. "It was only that night when I realized how much my bones ached!"

Focus, Daisy told herself as the crew prepared to start the scene again.

Kyle winked at her. "We'll get it right this time."

When the director called for action, Daisy opened the hood of the car. Steam was pouring out from the engine. She smiled broadly, leaned over, and closed her eyes.

"What are you doing?" Kyle asked.

"I could use a facial," Daisy answered, turning her head to the left and right, before she started to cough.

"What's a facial?"

The director smiled as he watched the action on a video screen. When the scene was over he yelled, "Cut!" and jumped out of his chair. "That's it!"

Daisy's throat felt dry from breathing the artificial smoke. The makeup girl handed her a bottle of water, then patted her face with a sponge. They did the scene two more times. While the crew was moving the camera from one side of the car to the other, Daisy snuck a look at her cell phone.

Cleo still hadn't called back.

I thought it felt lousy when I checked my phone to see if a certain guy had called and he hadn't, Daisy thought. That's nothing compared to the emptiness I feel right now. Cleo didn't want to tell me that she was leaving the house because she wanted me to concentrate on the movie. I'm trying, Cleo, Daisy thought. But who made you leave? And where did you go? Did you tell me anything that might give a hint? Cleo, you're my best friend, I should remember something you told me that might help Regan Reilly find you.

Please be OK, Cleo. Please.

57

The guy who wanted to buy Edna's sideboard was middle-aged, dressed in a cheap suit, and had an affected air. He gave Regan the creeps.

"I didn't see anything else at all in your home that interests me, Mrs. Frawley," he said disdainfully. "It's the sideboard or nothing."

"Nothing!" Edna stated. "Please leave! You are rude and insulting."

"Well, excuse me!" He turned and charged out the door.

Jody tried to make amends. "I'm sorry," she said. "Sometimes people say they don't want to sell something but for the right price . . ."

Oh sure, Regan thought. I bet you're making a percentage on everything that's sold.

Regan conferred with Edna and Nora, then she went up to Karen's room, shut the door, and called Jack.

"I'm getting there!" he said when he answered the phone. "Maybe another twenty minutes."

Regan smiled. "Great. Come straight to Edna's house," she said, speaking quietly. Shoppers were outside in the hallway.

191

Quickly she explained to him the latest developments. "You said you wanted to help?"

"Anything for you."

"I'd love for your office to run a check on Cleo's agent's son. Maybe the agent, too. They claim to not know where Cleo is, and maybe they don't, but I'm afraid if the son ran into her there would be trouble. He was furious when he left here."

"What are their names?"

"Ronald Flake and Horace Flake. Horace is the son."

"I'll call the office right away," Jack said.

After they hung up, Regan sat for a moment. *I doubt Cleo went back to Los Angeles but it wouldn't hurt to call her apartment building out there.* Regan searched the Internet and found the name of the management company for Cleo's building, then called their main number. Naturally she heard an automated recording that listed all her options. She pressed 0 for the operator and heard another recording. *What does it take to get a human being to answer the phone?* she wondered with frustration.

Three more tries.

"May I help you?" the operator asked.

"Yes, I'd like to speak to the manager of Kings Way."

The operator didn't feel the need to respond. She connected Regan to an extension without saying a word. A woman's voice mail picked up. "Hi. This is Alicia Isabella Jurcisin. I'm not at my desk right now but . . ."

Regan left a message for Alicia to please call her back. Next Regan tried to reach the operator again. This time it took four tries.

"Hello," Regan began when the operator picked up. "I was just connected to the manager of Kings Way but she's not there.

Can you give me the number of the superintendent of that building?"

"One moment."

Regan waited.

"The number of the office in that building is 323 . . ."

"And the superintendent's name?" Regan asked.

"Rufus Spells."

"Thank you." Regan hung up and dialed the number. Why am I not surprised to hear another voice mail message? she wondered.

"Hello, this is Rufus Spells. I will be away until August 8th. If you need help, please call Alicia Isabella Jurcisin at . . ."

Regan hung up. I'll have to wait and see if Alicia calls me back. And I really would like to speak to Daisy when she's free. But now it's time to do another Internet search of Cleo Paradise. When I looked her up this morning I only read the first few entries. I had no idea I'd become so interested in learning more about her. She typed in Cleo's name.

Scrolling down, Regan had dozens of articles to choose from. She clicked on one that caught her eye. "Cleo's super not thrilled with her movie."

Rufus aka Dizzy Spells was shocked by the way Cleo Paradise mimicked his mannerisms for her role as the nutty super in My Super Super. *He felt like he was being made fun of and refused to speak with us. We caught him on camera carrying a trash can of re-cyclables to the curb. Click on the video to watch his reaction.*

Oh brother, Regan thought as she accessed the video. Dizzy did have an awkward walk, but he was whistling while he worked. There was a sweetness about his demeanor. Sweet until the cameraman called out to him, "Hey, Dizzy, stick out your tongue for us the way Cleo did in the movie."

Dizzy glanced up at the camera, suddenly furious. He looked like he wanted to throw the garbage can. Instead he turned around and carried it back inside the building.

I guess he has reason to dislike Cleo, Regan thought. I wish I'd seen the movie. She scrolled down for more articles and learned that Cleo loved to read and swim and walk on the beach. Not go in the ocean, though, Regan remembered. Judson said she'd been knocked over by a wave and it had really scared her.

Regan then searched the Net for more about Dizzy. A video of him had just been posted from the Jersey Shore!

Regan watched as Dizzy tried to put up a beach umbrella. She listened carefully to the voice-over, obviously narrated by a teenaged boy. "Caught on tape—*the Super Super*! My friends and I recorded this guy putting up his beach umbrella because it was so funny to watch. Look at him spill that suntan lotion all over himself. We had no idea who this dude was but he made us laugh. Then a plane with a banner flies by and his wife starts yelling at him about Cleo Paradise . . . Boy, did he get mad! See the plane? That's when we figured out he was Cleo's super! Look at him storm off! Lighten up, Dizzy. We think you're *super*! This is brought to you from Seaside Heights at the Jersey Shore. August 4th."

Oh my God, Regan thought. He's nearby.

58

Inside a bank lobby on the Upper West Side of Manhattan, Scott filled out a deposit slip, and got on line behind a delivery boy with a large bag of coins. When it was Scott's turn, the number 13 was blinking on a board that indicated the next free window. He smiled and headed over.

"Hello." The teller stared straight at him, her gray eyes cold.

"Hello." Scott nervously slid the deposit slip and the check under the partition that separated them.

The teller looked at both sides of the check several times and studied the deposit slip. She turned to her computer and started tapping away at the keyboard. The whole process was agonizing for Scott. He felt as if he'd passed a note demanding all the money in the bank. Finally she punched the check and the deposit slip in a machine, and handed him his receipt. "Thank you."

"Thank you." Scott turned and made a beeline for the exit. Get me out of here, he thought. When he returned to his car, he felt euphoric. Impulsively he decided to call Hayley. He picked up his phone, found her name in his contact list, and was about to press send when a call came through. It was Jillian.

"Hey," he said.

"Where are you? Did you meet with the Binders?" she asked.

"No, they cancelled. How's it going at the Petrone garage sale?"

"Not good," she said. "Not good at all."

59

Hayley had been sitting in the trendy rooftop restaurant with Carwood Douglas, producer of the upcoming celebrity therapist show, and his group of fawning assistants, for over an hour.

"I have a thought," Carwood pronounced. "At the party we should hand out little notebooks and pens. We'll tell everyone to pretend they're shrinks and to ask others how they feel. It would be quite the icebreaker, don't you think? And of course there would be couches everywhere. Couches and tissue boxes."

"Wow, that's fabulous," one of his assistants enthused.

"Brilliant," another opined. "Absolutely brilliant."

"Hayley?" Carwood asked, tilting his champagne glass toward her.

Hayley cleared her throat. "My feelings are that it would definitely work."

"Your feelings! How divine!" Carwood snapped his fingers. "Waiter, let's have another bottle of champagne. Hayley, you are the perfect person to plan my soiree."

Something tells me this guy will never have a party, Hayley thought. He just wants to talk about it. "We'll make it a smash," she said, hedging her bets.

"Hayley"—Carwood leaned toward her—"you want to know the biggest lesson I learned after years and years of therapy?"

"Of course."

"What doesn't kill me only makes me stronger. Don't you agree?"

"I do." And after the day I've had, I should be Hercules, Hayley thought, accepting a glass of champagne from the waiter. I'm dying to get out of here, and I can't wait to talk to Regan. She still doesn't know that the newly engaged Scott asked me out for Saturday.

If only she could have followed him tonight.

60

I hate you, Cleo Paradise.
You think you can fool me by running away to a log cabin camp?
You can't.
I'm right here!
Come out, come out, wherever you are.

61

Dirk had a firm grip on Cleo's hand. "Nope, I'm not letting you go." He looked up at her, smiling.

For a second Cleo felt unsure. I'm in this guy's cabin, I don't really know him, and he's holding my hand a little too tight. No one who cares about me has any idea where I am. I must be nuts. A million thoughts went running through Cleo's mind. I'm registered under an assumed name. He could kill me and get away with it.

Dirk softened his grip, then dropped her hand, turning his attention to his ankle. He winced as he adjusted the bag of ice. "This is starting to melt. Would you mind making a fresh one?"

I'm too paranoid, Cleo told herself. Way too paranoid. This poor guy is in pain. I just spoke to his mother. What does it take for me to trust someone? "Of course," she said quickly. "You're sure you don't want to have that ankle checked out by a doctor?"

"I'm positive."

62

Regan replayed the video of Dizzy Spells on the beach. He looked so angry when he stormed off, fueled by a fight with his wife about Cleo Paradise. Wilted flowers had been left for Cleo in Los Angeles, then in New Jersey. Could it have been Spells? If so, what might he do next? Daisy would know how much trouble Cleo actually had with him. Regan dialed Daisy's number but reached her voice mail. She left a message, then tried the manager of Kings Way again.

Regan was amazed when a human voice answered.

"Hi, this is Alicia Jurcisin."

"Alicia, my name is Regan Reilly. I left you a message before. I'm at the Jersey Shore and I understand that Rufus Spells is here in Seaside Heights."

"He'll be back at work on Monday," Alicia said evasively.

"I used to live in Los Angeles but I moved to New York. I'd love to see Dizzy while he's here," Regan explained, trying to give the impression they were old buddies. "Can you give me his cell phone number?"

"I'm sorry, but I can't."

"I understand perfectly. Do you by any chance have the name of the hotel he's staying at?"

"He's not at a hotel. He's staying with his wife's family."

"Oh, how nice," Regan said. "His wife, yes, her name is . . ."

"Monique."

"I don't suppose you could give me their number, could you? I'd hate to miss the chance to see them."

"I'm sorry, but I'm not at liberty to give out a private number, either. If you'd like, I'll take your number and send Dizzy a text message on his phone."

"I'd appreciate that. My name, again, is Regan Reilly and my number is . . ."

"I'll see he gets it," Alicia said.

"Thanks so much." Regan hung up, doubtful that she'd ever hear from him. *He doesn't know who I am. And when he gets wind of the latest online video he won't be in a great mood. He'll have more reason to be furious with Cleo. If he's the one who's been leaving her the flowers, that really isn't good.*

Regan typed Rufus's name into the search box on her Black-Berry again and added the name "Monique" to her search. *If I could only find her maiden name,* Regan thought. Finally she did—a picture of Monique at a high school reunion. Monique Cammarizzo Spells.

Regan started searching for Cammarizzo in Seaside Heights, New Jersey.

There was a knock at the door.

"Come in," Regan said, still focused on her BlackBerry, her back to the door. "There's the address," she murmured. "But the phone is unlisted." She was about to get up when a pair of arms encircled her.

"Oh!" Regan gasped, then laughed as Jack leaned down and kissed her hello. "It's you."

"Who'd you think it would be?"

"I don't know. Maybe a crazy shopper who wanted this chair."

She leaned her head against his. "Don't get comfortable. We've got to hit the road."

"Where are we going?"

"Seaside Heights."

"Who's in Seaside Heights?"

"Cleo's super. I don't think he'll be happy to see us."

63

I've had enough, Wilbur thought. He and Stix had been in a dark, dingy, smoke-filled casino for hours. Stix had gone straight to the craps tables, while Wilbur tried his hand at the slot machines. He'd limited himself to betting one hundred dollars. When it was all gone, he walked around the floor several times, then found his way back to the table where Stix was still playing.

"Stix, what do you say we head home?"

"Listen, Wilbur," Stix barked, "if you don't want to spend time with me, that's fine. Go running to Edna. See if I care."

"Edna has nothing to do with it," Wilbur said. "I'd be happy to go someplace else. I feel as if I really need some fresh air. Let's take a walk on the Boardwalk."

Stix looked at his watch. "I promise we'll leave here in an hour."

"You mind if I go outside?" Wilbur asked.

"Be my guest."

Wilbur crossed the casino floor, past rows and rows of blinking, buzzing, blaring slot machines. He wasn't feeling great. Outside there was no breeze and it was unbearably hot. When he reached the Boardwalk, he sat down on a bench, pulled out his phone, and called Edna.

"Wilbur!" Edna cried. "How's your day?"

"It's okay," he said, trying to sound upbeat. "How's your sale?"

"Pretty good. But, Wilbur," Edna whispered, "there's a problem with Cleo Paradise. Her parents don't know where she is. She might be in trouble."

"That's a shame," Wilbur said, feeling a heaviness in his chest.

Edna filled him in on how surprised she was when Nora Regan Reilly showed up with her daughter, who was a private investigator. "And now Regan is on the hunt for Cleo!"

"Edna, I knew you couldn't have an ordinary garage sale," Wilbur joked. "Something peculiar always happens when you're around."

"I hope you mean that in a good way."

"You know I do, sweetie. Well, I just thought I'd say hello."

"Where are you?"

"I'm out on the Boardwalk. Stix is in the casino. I'm going back in and try to talk him into leaving. I'd like to get home and take a nap. I'll call you later. 'Bye . . ." Wilbur closed his phone and got up. Slowly he walked back toward the casino, which was a block away. I feel so tired, he thought. Well, what do I expect? I'm eighty years old.

Expecting a protest from Stix, Wilbur was thrilled to hear that he was ready to go. But his gambling friend didn't look happy. They walked out to the parking lot and got in Stix's car.

"I should have quit while I wasn't so far behind," Stix muttered as he started up the engine.

"Stix, I'm feeling a little under the weather. You mind if I shut my eyes for a few minutes?"

"Not at all. I'll turn on the ball game."

He probably has a bet on it, Wilbur thought as he pushed back his seat and fell fast asleep.

64

Regan and Jack went downstairs and found Nora in the gazebo. Edna was in the yard speaking on a cordless phone.

Nora smiled at Jack. "My favorite son-in-law located my daughter?"

"I did," Jack said. "And she's already put me to work."

In hushed tones, Regan explained where they were going.

"Her super is here at the Shore?" Nora said, adjusting her sunglasses. "That's certainly interesting."

"And he's not Cleo's number one fan." Regan turned to Jack. "You should have seen the couple who were first in line today. The president and vice president of Cleo's fan club. What a pair of winners."

"They were beauts," Nora agreed.

"Mom," Regan whispered, looking around to make sure Edna was out of earshot. "Are you sure you can't go home now?"

Nora shook her head. "I'm not leaving. In for a penny, in for a pound, as they say. That Jody is a little pushy for my taste."

"Mine, too. Karen really owes you one."

"She does."

"When is Dad getting down?"

"At about seven."

"I don't know when we'll see you," Regan said, then shrugged. "With any luck Cleo will call soon and tell us she's fine."

"I'm praying for her," Nora said simply.

A chill went through Regan's body. Hearing her mother say those words made the whole situation feel more dire.

"Okayyyy," Edna said, stepping into the gazebo, the wireless phone in her hand. "That was my fella. He's down in Atlantic City."

"Everything all right?" Nora asked. "You look worried."

Edna frowned as she took a seat. "He didn't sound quite like himself. He said he wants to get back home and take a nap, which is unlike him. I'm sure he'll be fine," she said, trying to brush off her concern. "Jack, can I get you anything?"

"No, thank you. We're on our way."

Again, Regan quickly explained where they were going. "Edna, I know you didn't see Cleo much. But if you think of anything she said, or anything you found around the house that might give us an idea of where she went, please let me know."

"I will, Regan. I promise." Edna's demeanor had turned so serious, as if the worry over her boyfriend had finally made her wake up to the fact that Cleo could be in real danger.

Out in his car, Jack programmed the GPS for the Cammarizzos' address in Seaside Heights. They started to pull down Edna's street when Regan's phone rang. It was Hayley.

"Regan, I've been dying to talk to you. I have something to tell you you're not going to believe."

"Same here," Regan said.

"You first," Hayley said.

"No, go ahead." Regan was happy to put off delivering more bad news.

"Okay. Ready?"

"Yes."

"Scott called and asked me out for Saturday night!"

"What?"

"You heard me. He actually had the nerve to tell me he'd been with his son last night."

"I can't believe it," Regan said, shaking her head.

"I knew you wouldn't. Of course I said yes. I have big plans for him. Now what's your news?"

Oy, Regan thought. Here goes. "After I spoke with you this morning my mother called and asked me to come with her to a garage sale at the shore."

"Don't tell me. You bought something that is worth a whole lot more than you paid for it. I love those stories."

"It's not that."

"Then what?"

"Scott's fiancée was working at the sale," Regan said, then wisely held the phone out from her ear.

"His fiancée?"

"Yes."

"Where's the sale? I'll call a car service right now."

"She's not there anymore. She went off to run another sale."

"I can't believe this!" Hayley said. "Tell me every detail. What do you mean she went off to run another sale?"

"She's in business with another woman. They help people with garage sales, higher-end ones, I guess."

Hayley was hyperventilating. "How can I compete with that?" she asked sarcastically. "Obviously Scott likes women who plan events!"

"I guess he does."

"Does she have another big garage sale Saturday night, and he has nothing to do? Is that why he wants to see me?"

"I don't know, Hayley. It's a good question." Regan paused. "She wasn't wearing an engagement ring."

"That doesn't mean anything," Hayley said. "It might not have fit."

"That's true."

"Or maybe she hated the ring and is making him change it."

"Always a possibility."

"But I want to find out what's going on with this guy! You thought I was mad this morning? Regan, what's the name of their business?"

"Hayley, be careful."

"Regan, Scott asked me out again! This situation has not been put to rest. I'm not prolonging the agony. *He* is. And he's going to pay for it! What's the name of their business? Oh wait! What's her name?"

"Jillian. Her partner's name is Jody. I don't know their last names."

"And the name of their business?"

"Garage Sale Gurus."

"Oh please!"

"I'll help you, Hayley, but right now I have something else going on." Regan explained about Cleo Paradise.

"Cleo Paradise? I just saw her archenemy at lunch today."

"Her archenemy? Who's that?"

"An actress named April Dockton. Cleo beat her out for the part in *My Super Super*. The producer I had lunch with said if she were Cleo, she wouldn't want to meet April in a dark alley."

65

When Kit went back into her office building, she stopped at the newsstand in the lobby. The headline of a popular woman's magazine caught her eye.

"Three words to describe why you will never ever ever get married. PICKY PICKY PICKY. Who do you think you are anyway?"

Oh swell, Kit thought. It's the old blame-the-victim. Whenever people told her she was too picky, she'd point out to them that a guy she was dating and thought she wanted to marry turned into a psycho and tried to kill her—and her best friend. So there! I wasn't picky enough. I overlooked signs that he was a deranged killer just so I could have a relationship. She avoided mentioning that he was also extremely handsome and very rich.

Against her better judgment, Kit bought the magazine. I must be a masochist, she thought. I can predict with 100 percent accuracy what the article will say—someone like me deserves to be alone because I don't give someone like Winston a chance. Well, the weekend's about to begin and I'm alone. But so is Regan's client and you can't blame *her* for being picky! The lowlife she was dating got engaged to someone else and hadn't told her yet.

Kit returned to her office, the magazine in a brown bag which she stuck in her bottom drawer. *The last thing I need is for anyone in this joint to see that screaming headline. I'll never live it down.*

As the afternoon wore on, Kit couldn't get the word "picky" out of her mind. *Maybe, just maybe, I should give Winston a call,* she mused. *What's wrong with a friendly hello? Maybe I should give him another chance. If he'll even let me. He called me three times the night after our date, asking if I'd gotten home to Connecticut safely. I never called him back. He is obviously thoughtful. He even made a special trip to a garage sale to buy something of Cleo's for his sister. And it's kind of cute that he bought goldfish bowls and a fish tank. Regan and Jack were impressed when they met him on the beach. Oh, I don't know,* Kit wavered. *He carries vinegar in his beach bag. I'm not sure I can get past that. And his nonstop talk about invertebrates was excruciating. I shouldn't let that headline about being picky influence my better judgment. But still . . .*

A coworker poked his head in her door. "Kit, we're about to start the meeting."

"I'm ready," Kit said, getting up. *My internal debate about calling Winston will have to wait. I'll ask Regan what she thinks. But right now she has much more important things to worry about. Could Cleo Paradise really be in danger? Is whoever left the dead flowers out to get her?*

Kit shivered, remembering how terrified she was when her wacko beau tried to kill her. *I was never so scared in my life.*

Please, God, don't let something like that happen to Cleo, Kit prayed. *Help Regan find her before it's too late.*

66

————◆————

Ronald Flake was disgusted. He'd stood in the parking lot at the train station where he'd been so rudely thrown out of Horace's car, sure that his son would be right back. It was only when the train came roaring down the tracks that Ronnie ran to the ticket counter and forked over his money. He'd boarded the train in disbelief, taken a seat in a nearly empty car, and tried to call his son.

Horace didn't pick up.

I cannot believe he would do this to me, Ronnie fumed, shaking the phone in his hand. My own flesh and blood is a loser beyond words. It all comes from his mother's side of the family. Ronnie waited for the beep on Horace's voice mail, then whispered into the phone. "Son, you're just like your crazy Uncle Noogie who's rotting in prison." He hung up, then quickly called back. "Son, I hate to admit it but you were a big mistake." When he disconnected the second time, an idea sprung to mind. Smiling broadly, Ronnie dialed again.

Ronnie left message after insulting message until Horace's mailbox was full.

67

Jack's office called as he and Regan entered the town of Seaside Heights.

"Yes, Keith," Jack said to his assistant as he put the call on the speakerphone so Regan could listen in to the conversation. "What have you got for me?"

"Horace Flake has been arrested several times for assault. He's an unlicensed taxi driver and has been in and out of jail over the past twenty years."

"Where does he live?"

"In Queens with his parents."

"How about the father?"

"Ronald Flake has never been arrested but he's been sued by four clients in the last eight years for not paying them in full."

"Thanks," Jack said.

"Let me know if you need anything else."

"I will. Talk to you later."

"Poor Cleo," Regan said as Jack disconnected the call. "I'd want to get away from the Flakes, too. I'm hoping this means that Cleo is just retreating from the world for a while."

Jack turned onto a narrow street off the main road. Small but neat beach cottages lined the block. Clotheslines hung in tiny front yards that consisted of smooth white pebbles. No one was around. They found the Cammarizzo home and parked in front.

"Here we go," Regan said.

As they got out of the car, the front door of the Cammarizzos' opened.

"Be right back!" A frazzled, attractive fortyish woman emerged from the house, car keys in hand. She had light brown hair and was wearing aqua blue terry cloth shorts and a white sleeveless shirt. Clearly she was in a hurry.

"Excuse me," Regan called across the small yard.

"What?"

"I was wondering if Dizzy is home . . ."

"No, that jerk is not home. He had a fight with my cousin and left her stranded at the beach with the three kids. Nice, huh? I'm going to pick them up now. That guy uses up all the hot water in the house, then he has the nerve to complain about me? I hope he drops dead." She got in her car, backed out of the driveway, then hit the gas, sending stray pebbles flying.

Regan and Jack looked at each other.

"If I were Dizzy I might never come back," Regan said.

Jack shook his head. "I can't say I blame him."

"Why don't we pull the car down to the end of the block and wait for a while?" Regan suggested. "Maybe he'll appear."

68

Well hello," Rhonda said, greeting Striker and Harriet as they straggled in the door of her restaurant. "I never see you here this early. It's still light out!"

"We've had a bad day," Striker grunted.

"A really bad day," Harriet agreed. "It's all my fault. We needed to get out of the house. But we also wanted to congratulate you on your engagement."

Rhonda smiled. "Word spreads fast. I'm so happy. I can't wait for you to meet Frankie. Let's have a drink," she said, leading them to a table in the front near the window. "Sit and relax."

Striker and Harriet sank into their chairs, while Rhonda signaled for a waitress. "Peggy, we'd like to order drinks, please."

"Right away."

After they placed their order, Rhonda folded her hands in front of her. "So. Do you want to tell me about your bad day? Or would you rather try and forget it?"

Harriet rolled her eyes. "I'd better tell you so you don't end up making the same mistake."

"Now I'm really curious."

"Well," Harriet began. "I got the bright idea to clean out our house, get rid of the clutter, and have a garage sale. I don't know how to run a sale so I hired a company that helps you with every detail. A woman came to clear out our clutter . . ." She paused, starting to choke on her words.

Striker put his arm around her. "It's okay, honey."

Harriet shook her head. "No it's not. Anyway, she convinced me to throw out so many of our personal things that we really would have liked to keep forever. Flowers Striker gave me . . ." She blinked back tears.

"My baseball cards," Striker added.

"You collected baseball cards?" Rhonda asked. "They can be valuable."

"Don't remind me. Baseball and music are my two loves. Besides Harriet."

Harriet tried to smile. "Striker, I'm so glad you didn't realize those cards were gone until after she left today. I've never seen you so angry."

"You saw this woman today?" Rhonda asked.

"Yes," Harriet answered. "Our garage sale was this afternoon. It wasn't exactly mobbed. What a waste of our time and money."

"If I ever see that woman again . . . ," Striker said, shaking his head.

Rhonda looked thoughtful and was about to say something when the waitress placed their drinks on the table.

Striker lifted his glass of beer. "To your engagement, Rhonda. Frankie's a lucky guy. We're thrilled for you."

"We certainly are," Harriet agreed, raising her piña colada.

"Thank you," Rhonda said as they all clinked glasses. She took a sip of her wine, then yawned. "I'm a little tired because I was up really late last night celebrating with my friends. It was so much fun. Everyone in the restaurant was congratulating me, even customers I had never met before. It's funny how friendly strangers become in certain situations. They let their guard down. It reminded me of when people smile and make faces at somebody's baby in an elevator."

"A friend of mine meets more girls when he goes to the park with his dog than when he goes to bars," Striker said.

Harriet grinned. "That guy is too much. His poor dog is exhausted. Did you ever meet a dog that didn't want to go for a walk?"

They all laughed.

"You guys are great," Rhonda said. "Forget the garage sale. But it's funny. Frankie just called before. His mother is having a garage sale today, too."

"Frankie grew up around here, right?" Striker asked quickly.

"Yes, in Bay Head."

"Does his mother still live there?"

"Yes."

"Did Cleo Paradise rent her house recently?"

"Yes. How did you know?"

"How did I know?" Striker asked, his expression astonished. "The company we hired was in charge of that sale as well!"

"The same company?" Rhonda asked, her eyes widening.

"Yes! And your fiancé's mother took out an ad in the paper and hired a plane to fly over the beach with one of those banners."

Rhonda's jaw dropped. "I never looked at the newspaper today . . ."

"Well, I hope Frankie didn't have any baseball cards he wanted to save," Striker said. "Because with that lousy company in charge, you can be sure they're long gone."

69

Regan and Jack had been waiting in the car for over an hour, and there was no sign of Dizzy or his family. If the woman from the management company had sent Dizzy Regan's message, he'd obviously ignored it.

Finally Daisy called back. "I just got free," she said breathlessly. "Regan, do you have any news?"

"Cleo's parents called from Europe. They couldn't get in touch with her today, either, and are on their way back."

"Oh no," Daisy said softly. "This is not good."

"I have to ask you about Cleo's super," Regan said, then explained where she was. "I'm surprised he's here at the Jersey Shore."

"Ever since Cleo met Dizzy he talked about the Jersey Shore and how much he loved it. That's why Cleo decided to rent a house there."

"Was he angry with her about the movie?"

"Not at first. He and Cleo had always been friendly. But so many people started to get mean and make fun of his klutziness after they'd seen the movie. He told Cleo he felt like he was under a microscope. All the teasing started to get to him. The nickname 'Dizzy' didn't help matters. Now there's a video on the

Internet of him trying to put up a beach umbrella? Oh boy. Wait till Cleo hears about this. She felt bad about the way the whole thing snowballed. It was getting really uncomfortable for her in the building. Dizzy's wife, Monique, was never very nice to her and after the movie came out things got worse. Cleo's lease is up in October and she'd started looking for another place to live."

"Monique wasn't nice to Cleo?"

"Not really. Cleo's a beautiful girl. When she moved into the building two years ago, Dizzy was constantly running to help her, which I'm sure annoyed Monique. After the movie came out, all the attention, positive and negative, really bugged her. A magazine wanted to do a photo shoot with Cleo and Dizzy but his wife put the kibosh on it. Monique isn't a fan of Cleo's, that's for sure."

"Does Cleo have a fan club?"

"Not an official fan club. Why?"

"A couple people came to the garage sale today who said they were president and vice president of Cleo Paradise's fan club."

"I can't wait to tell Cleo that," Daisy said, her voice starting to tremble. "You have to find her, Regan, so I can tell her that."

"I know," Regan answered quietly. "Was Dizzy aware Cleo had rented a place at the Shore?"

"Yes. She always tried to chat with him, but things weren't the same lately. When Cleo told him about our plans to go to the Jersey Shore he just said, 'Oh, that's nice,' and walked away. Regan, I'm trying to think of something that Cleo said that could help you find her. I thought she might have started driving to Florida, but we'll be doing so much driving later that doesn't make sense. I was planning to fly into Newark. My guess is she probably stayed in the area, but where could she have gone?"

"The guy who takes care of the pool at Mrs. Frawley's house thought Cleo probably wouldn't look for another place near the beach. She told him she'd been knocked over by a wave and it scared her."

"She told me that, too. It was late in the afternoon after the lifeguards had left. She said she never would swim in the ocean alone again. If I'd been there, we probably would have gone to the beach a lot," Daisy said wistfully. "Regan, I think Cleo would want to find somewhere quiet, and I don't think she'd want to be holed up in a hotel. She likes to jog. And she certainly liked to go camping with her parents. Oh, I don't know."

"Daisy, I just spoke to a friend of mine who told me that she had lunch today in a restaurant in New York City. The actress April Dockton was also at the restaurant—"

"April Dockton!" Daisy interrupted. "She hates Cleo! She just worked on the movie I'm doing and had to try and strangle me in a scene. She wasn't acting, I'll tell you that."

Oh great, Regan thought. "I don't suppose you have her phone number, then."

"No. Do you want me to try and get it? Someone in production here must have it."

"Sure. I don't know yet what my pretense for calling her would be, but I'll think of something." Then Regan told Daisy about the episode with the Flakes.

"Flake's son is a nutcase! He asked Cleo out a number of times but she always turned him down. When she lived in New York City, he'd call and offer to drive her to auditions. Cleo couldn't stand him."

"I can understand why," Regan said. "He doesn't exactly ooze charm. Daisy, if you can get April's number, call me back."

"I will, Regan. And I'll keep thinking."

70

Wilbur opened his eyes when the car stopped moving. He felt like he'd been asleep for a while. "Where are we?" he asked Stix, checking his watch and looking around. It was six o'clock. They were in the parking lot of a small diner on a rural road. The opposite side of the street was heavily wooded.

Stix didn't answer. "I have to ask you a favor," he growled, his expression tense.

Wilbur was baffled. "What?"

"I've got to run an errand. Would you mind waiting in the diner? Go in and have a cup of coffee."

"A cup of coffee? Stix, I want to go home."

"Please, this is important," Stix said. "I promise I'll be right back."

"How long will it take us to get home from here?"

"Don't worry about it. Hurry up, Wilbur."

"I never in all my life," Wilbur said, shaking his head. He opened the door and struggled to lift himself out of the seat. Still feeling lousy, he longed to be home, stretched out on his couch. Gingerly he stepped out onto the pavement and shut the door. Stix pulled out of the parking lot without a backward glance.

The air was so still and quiet except for the sound of the crickets.

Wilbur turned. He took one step, then collapsed onto the ground.

71

"Here they are," Regan said as Monique's cousin's car drove past. "You know, Jack, it's been hours and Cleo still hasn't returned my call. Who knows when Dizzy will show up? I have to at least try to get his wife to talk to me."

"Let's do it," Jack said. He turned the key in the engine and drove down the block. When they parked in front of the Cammarizzos', the boys had already run inside the house. Monique and her cousin were unloading bags of groceries from the trunk.

Monique's cousin looked up as Regan and Jack got out of the car. "I told you Dizzy wasn't here. What do you want now?"

"I'm Dizzy's wife. Why are you looking for him?" Monique asked suspiciously, her face flashing with anger.

"We're actually trying to track down Cleo Paradise," Regan explained. "I'm a private investigator. Cleo's parents haven't heard from her lately and are worried. She left the house she was renting here at the Shore last Friday. We were wondering if she'd been to her apartment in Los Angeles. Perhaps your husband could call people in the building to see if anyone's seen her this week."

"Give me a break," Monique said, shaking her head. "Dizzy's

on vacation. Why should he have to worry about Cleo's disappearing act?"

"I didn't say anything about a disappearing act," Regan said firmly. "Cleo's parents are worried, and I'm trying to explore every avenue. You're a mother, you must understand. Can you try and reach your husband for me?"

"He doesn't have his phone with him."

"Do you know where he is?"

"No. We were at the beach and he left. I don't know when he'll be back."

"Monique, I told them he stranded you there, the jerk."

"Sheryl!" Monique snapped. "Keep your opinion about my husband to yourself."

"This has been some vacation," Sheryl muttered.

"Do you have the name of anyone in your building in Los Angeles that I could call and find out if they've seen Cleo this past week?" Regan asked.

Monique shrugged.

"I'll say it again. Cleo's parents are desperately worried. If one of your children went missing, no matter how old they might be, you'd feel—"

"Okay!" Monique interrupted. "When we travel, Dizzy always brings a list of the people who live in the building and their numbers. You can make the calls. I don't have time."

"That's fine."

"But I don't know whether I should be giving out this information to total strangers."

Jack pulled out his badge.

"Oh," Monique said quickly. "All right, then."

One of the boys, who'd been watching from the window, came running out the door. "Hey, mister, let me see your badge. Are you a real police officer?"

"Yes, I am," Jack said with a smile, crouching down.

"I saw a bad guy once," the boy reported, his eyes shining with excitement.

"You did?" Jack asked.

"Tommy, what are you talking about?" Monique demanded.

"I was outside our building. The bad guy pulled up on a motorcycle and threw ugly flowers on this lady Cleo's car. I thought that was mean."

"When did this happen?" Monique asked.

"I don't know."

"You should have told Mommy and Daddy."

"But you said you didn't want to hear one more word about Cleo Paradise. *Not one more word.*"

Out of the mouths of babes, Regan thought.

Monique groaned. "I'll get the list. Come on, Tommy."

"But, Mommy!"

"Hey, buddy," Jack said kindly. "Do as your mother tells you." He held out his hand. "But first give me five."

Tommy squealed with delight. He drew back his skinny little arm then slapped his hand as hard as he could into Jack's palm.

"Way to go," Jack said, then patted Tommy's head.

Reluctantly Tommy followed his mother and their scowling cousin into the house. A minute later, Monique came back out with a sheet of paper. "Take this. Dizzy keeps extra copies."

"Thank you," Regan said. "Would you mind giving me your number?"

"My cell number is on there."

"Great," Regan said, then handed Monique her card. "Please have your husband call me when he returns. As you can see from what your son just told us, Cleo could be in danger. Maybe Cleo mentioned something in passing to your husband that could help us."

"Okay," Monique said.

Regan and Jack got back in the car. "Well, at least we know Dizzy didn't leave Cleo the flowers in Los Angeles," Regan said as she put on her seat belt.

"But who was the guy on the motorcycle?" Jack wondered aloud. "What do you want to do now, Regan?"

"Why don't we go back to Edna's? I'll start to make these calls. I'm sure Monique will have Dizzy call me when he gets back. If not, we'll pay them another visit later."

As Jack drove, Regan made call after call. No one she reached had seen Cleo.

"There's been a restaurant menu stuck halfway under her front door for days now," one of Cleo's neighbors reported. "I don't think she's been here."

"Thanks so much," Regan said, then hung up. "It's pretty clear Cleo hasn't been back to her apartment in Los Angeles."

"Daisy's probably right," Jack said. "Cleo most likely stayed somewhere not far from here."

Regan's phone rang. She glanced at the caller ID. "I don't know who this is," she said, then answered.

"Regan!" a woman shouted hysterically. "It's Edna!"

"Edna, what's wrong?" Regan asked quickly, afraid something had happened to Nora.

"They think Wilbur had a heart attack!" Edna sobbed. "He's in the emergency room in some godforsaken town in western New Jersey. Thank God my number was the last one he'd called from his cell phone. The hospital just called. Can you and Jack drive me out there? Please! Your mother said Jack has a special siren he can put on the car so we can get there as fast as possible. There's so much traffic . . ."

"Of course, Edna," Regan said. "We're two minutes away."

"Thank you, Regan. Thank you!"

MOBBED

Jack heard every word. He turned on the siren, stepped on the gas, and raced toward Edna's house. Nora and Edna were waiting at the curb. They jumped in the backseat.

"Hurry, Jack, please!" Edna wailed. "I'm so angry. Wilbur's rotten friend Stix dropped him off at a diner in the middle of nowhere to go run an errand. He knew Wilbur wasn't feeling well. God knows where Stix went! But I'll tell you this—when I get my hands on him, I'll wring his neck!"

72

After Judson finished mowing Old Man Appleton's lawn, the gnarly grump emerged from his house. Hands on hips, he glanced around the yard. "Good job."

"Thanks," Judson said, surprised at the compliment.

"My wife and I are having company this weekend. She just said we should have had our patio furniture cleaned. How about if we negotiate a price for you to do the job for us?"

"Sure thing, Mr. Appleton. I have a free window tomorrow."

"Tomorrow's too late. I need it done now. Our guests are arriving in the morning."

Judson was sweaty and tired and wanted to go home and have a beer. He decided he'd call Regan Reilly and tell her about the book Cleo Paradise had been reading. Old Man Appleton was difficult, but Judson didn't want to lose him as a client. The beer and the phone call would have to wait. "Okay, then, I'll do it now," Judson said agreeably.

Appleton cackled. "I thought you'd say yes. Let's walk over to the garage."

"The garage?"

"Yes. We've got half a dozen extra lounge chairs that need a good scrubbing. I want you to look at them before we decide on a price."

I'll never get out of here, Judson thought.

73

Jack had programmed the address of the hospital into the GPS and noted, "It's ninety-seven miles west."

"Ninety-seven miles!" Edna moaned.

Nora held Edna's hands in hers. "Everything will be okay," she said. "Jack will get us there quickly."

"Oh, Nora," Edna said woefully. "I suppose I should call Karen. She was taking a car service from the airport. I'm sure she's landed by now."

"Edna, what's her number?" Regan asked quickly, her phone in hand. "I'll get her on the line for you."

After one ring, Karen picked up. "Hello."

"Karen?"

"Yes."

"This is Nora Regan Reilly's daughter, Regan. Your mother is—"

"Oh, Regan," Karen interrupted. "I can't wait to meet you. I asked Nora to scout out my mother's garage sale today."

"I know—"

"My brother, Frankie, just called me," Karen continued excitedly. "His fiancée told him that the company who ran my mother's sale is questionable, at best. They threw out her friend's baseball cards. He had a garage sale today. Some of those baseball cards are worth a fortune. I just hope they didn't pull anything on us—"

"Karen, I'm not calling about the garage sale. We're on the way to the hospital. Your mother's boyfriend, Wilbur—"

"My mother's boyfriend?" Karen squealed. "I didn't know she had a boyfriend!"

"Yes, Wilbur was taken to a hospital with a possible heart attack," Regan said, avoiding commentary on Edna's love life. "My mother and I are bringing your mother there now."

"What hospital? Where?"

Regan told her, then handed the phone to Edna.

"Karen, I can't breathe, never mind talk," Edna said, crying. "Are you coming to the hospital?"

"Yes. I'm in the car now. I'll tell the driver."

"Thanks, honey. See you soon. 'Bye." Edna handed the phone back to Regan. "Regan, I'm sorry to interrupt your search for Cleo."

"It's okay, Edna. We'll get you to the hospital and take it from there."

Jack drove swiftly, his siren blaring as they headed for western New Jersey. The GPS instructed him to exit the main highway. They found themselves on a winding country road. The area became more and more rural. It was almost dark. They passed a sign for a log cabin camp—*the only one in New Jersey.*

Daisy said Cleo liked to go camping with her parents, Regan remembered. I've heard there are a lot of camps out this way by the Delaware Water Gap. Could Cleo have come all the way out here? Regan wondered.

When they reached the hospital, Jack pulled up in front of the emergency room entrance. "Go ahead in. I'll park the car."

Edna sprinted through the automatic doors. "Wilbur Parks!" she yelled to the receptionist. "Where is he?"

The receptionist frowned and turned to her computer screen. "I think they took him into surgery."

Edna yelped like a wounded animal, slumping against the desk. Regan and Nora had their arms around her.

"Oops," the receptionist said blandly, tapping her keys. "That's someone else. Mr. Parks is doing much better. You can go inside."

Edna yelped again, this time with relief. Regan and Nora followed her into a curtained-off area where Wilbur was sitting up in bed, an oxygen tube in his nose. "Wilbur," Edna cried. Tenderly she kissed his forehead. "How are you?"

Wilbur attempted to smile. "I've been better. But they say it wasn't a heart attack—I think it was too much time in a hot, smoky casino. At my age, I should know better."

"Oh, thank goodness."

"Edna," Nora said quietly, "we'll give you some privacy."

"No! Let me introduce you. Wilbur, these are my new friends Nora and Regan Reilly. They're better friends than that louse Stix. Where is he?"

"He called and said he had a family emergency. Oh look, here he is."

All heads turned as Stix approached. His shoes were muddy, his expression guilty.

Edna's nostrils flared. She stepped toward Stix and gave him a shove. "What's wrong with you?" she demanded.

"What are you talking about?" he whined.

"You leave Wilbur high and dry like that? What kind of errand did you have to do all the way out here?" Edna demanded. "Answer me!"

"I had a family situation," Stix insisted. "My cousin is really sick and his wife doesn't want any strangers around. I thought

I'd only be gone a few minutes." Stix started to cry. "My cousin's sick. Now Wilbur. I feel terrible."

Crocodile tears, Regan thought.

"Get out of here!" Edna shouted.

Stix looked over at Wilbur for support. But he wasn't getting any.

"Do what the lady says," Wilbur said.

Edna shoved Stix again. "Get lost. Be on your way before you end up in one of the other beds in this room!"

Stix grabbed the railing of Wilbur's bed to prevent himself from falling. The wallet that had been hanging out of his side pocket fell to the ground. A wad of one-hundred-dollar bills spilled out.

"Look at all your money!" Edna cried, as Stix quickly bent over to retrieve it. "Aren't you rich."

"You told me you lost all your money today," Wilbur said, shaking his fist.

Stix turned, and stormed out.

Regan looked at Edna. "Did Stix know Cleo Paradise was renting your house?"

"Everybody knew, right, honey?" Wilbur asked.

Now Edna looked guilty. "Word got around, I suppose."

"I'll be right back," Regan said, making a quick exit. Jack was coming through the emergency room door. "Let's go," she said, grabbing his arm.

"Where?"

"The man getting in that car is the one who deserted Wilbur. It's just a hunch, but I want to follow him. Hurry. We can't let him get away."

74

When Stix pulled out of the hospital parking lot, he turned left.

"Good!" Regan said. "If he were heading back to Golden Peaks, he'd turn right."

"I'll try not to make it obvious that we're following him," Jack said as he pulled out onto the road and also turned left. "But I'll have to keep up. He's going pretty fast."

"Edna threw him out of the emergency room," Regan said. "I think the last thing he would expect is that anyone would follow him. Wilbur also told him to get lost."

The winding road had no streetlights. Regan told Jack she thought Stix seemed much too jumpy and on edge. He looked so nervous, and his shoes had mud all over them. He knew Cleo was staying at Edna's. There might be no connection between Stix and Cleo's disappearance; but he was certainly up to something out here.

Stix put on his left blinker. Jack kept his distance as Stix turned down a heavily wooded dirt road that was marked "DEAD END."

"I'll wait a minute," Jack said. "But I don't want him to get too far ahead."

Jack finally turned, then lowered his lights. He and Regan rode slowly down the dark, bumpy road; nothing but woods was on either side. After a few minutes they could see a lighted farmhouse and barn set back to the left. Several cars were parked straight ahead where the road ended. A large U-Haul truck was in the driveway, backed up to the barn door.

"I wonder what's inside that barn," Regan said.

"Let me make a call to the local police before we take a look."

A minute later, Regan and Jack got out of the car. Jack took Regan's hand. Carefully they walked toward the property. Voices floated out into the darkness from the barn. They crept up the driveway, then came around the side of the U-Haul to the open barn door.

Not a horse or a cow or a chicken was in sight. The contents of the barn were a garage sale junkie's dream.

"Any bargains?" Regan called out.

Scott, Jillian, Jody, Stix, the president and vice president of Cleo's fan club, and a couple other "shoppers" Regan recognized from Edna's garage sale looked up.

"What are you doing here?" Scott shouted. "Get out!" He rushed to close the barn door.

"I wouldn't do that," Jack said, pulling out his badge. "You might as well cooperate."

Regan stepped forward and pointed to a table covered with the skulls that belonged to Cleo's parents. "I see a lot of familiar pieces. I can't wait to have a look around. Oh, and look at those baseball cards. I think I can find their rightful owner."

A police siren could be heard in the distance.

The "President" of Cleo's fan club sank into one of Edna's chairs. He was wearing the same ill-fitting shirt he had on at Edna's. "I knew I shouldn't have gotten involved in this. I'll cooperate! Please! All I did was show up at the sales and buy what they'd told me to buy with the cash they gave me. Is that such a crime? Jody and Jillian are the guilty ones. They underprice everything at their sales and then resell them for a profit."

Regan shook her head in disgust, and pointed her finger at Scott. "You are a complete lowlife. Why did you have to string my friend Hayley along? You got engaged to Jillian last night and then made a date with Hayley for Saturday!"

"Engaged?" Jody screamed. "What are you talking about?"

"My husband and I followed Scott to a restaurant last night. He proposed to Jillian. Her ring was in a fortune cookie. It was so romantic."

"What?" Jody glared at Scott and Jillian. "Are you two double-crossing me?"

Now Regan was confused. "Double-crossing *you*?"

"Scott and Jillian aren't engaged!" Mr. President explained. "They're cousins! Cheating people at garage sales is their family business. Who knows what else? They're a little mob! These people are all related."

"Not engaged?" Regan asked.

"I hope not!" Jody spat. "Their grandmother and grandfather were brother and sister. I can tell they left me out of something. And I'll find out what it is!"

So will I, Regan thought. She pointed to Stix. "What is your part in this?"

Mr. President answered. "Stix was married to their great-aunt. He and Scott like to gamble together. He gave them the lead on the garage sale today."

The police car arrived, its red light slicing through the darkness. Two officers hurried up the driveway.

Regan's cell phone rang. Quickly she answered.

"Regan, it's Judson the landscaper."

"Yes, Judson."

"I wanted to tell you something about Cleo but I thought it might seem stupid."

"It's only stupid if you don't tell me."

"Okay, then. Cleo was reading a book by the pool. I asked her if she liked it. She said she loved it."

"Right," Regan said.

"Well, it was about a pioneer family who lived in a log cabin. Cleo said she envied their simple lifestyle. I don't know. I'm sorry, but—"

"Judson, don't be sorry. I'll call you back later." Regan tapped Jack's arm. "Jack, let's go."

"Now?"

"Yes. I have another hunch. But this one's more important. I have an idea of where we might find Cleo." She turned and started running down the muddy driveway.

75

The hours Cleo and Dirk spent together passed quickly. After lunch, they'd watched an old movie and several episodes of *Bonanza*. For dinner, she'd heated up frozen pizza and they'd opened a bottle of wine.

"I'd better get back to my cabin," Cleo finally said.

"Why?" Dirk asked. They were sitting next to each other on the couch. "Aren't you having a good time?"

More than a good time, Cleo thought. So good I don't know what to think. She smiled. "If I weren't enjoying myself, do you think I would have stayed this long?"

"Let's finish this wine first," Dirk said, emptying the bottle. "Then I promise I'll let you go." He smiled. "But only until to-morrow morning."

76

I don't know or care if this is a wild goose chase," Regan said as she and Jack got in the car, "but we have to check out the log cabin camp we passed down the road."

"I noticed it, too," Jack said as he started the engine.

"Daisy said Cleo liked camping. The landscaper just called and said Cleo loved the book she was reading about a pioneer family living in a log cabin. We have to follow any lead we get."

"I'm with you, Regan." He turned the car around, drove out to the winding rural road, and made a left. "As I recall it's about eight or ten miles from here," he said.

They kept a careful watch. The road was so dark. Finally they spotted the sign for the camp.

"There it is!" Regan said.

The camp was about a quarter mile off the main road. When Jack turned in to the parking lot, lights were visible from the main office.

They parked next to a white SUV with California plates. "I hope this is Cleo's car," Regan said as they got out and hurried toward the office.

The sign on the door indicated it was open until ten o'clock.

A woman who appeared to be in her sixties was the only one inside.

"May I help you?" she asked.

"I hope so. My name is Regan Reilly. I'm a private investigator. This is my husband, Jack, who is with the NYPD." They both showed their I.D.s.

"What's wrong?" she asked.

"We're looking for the actress Cleo Paradise. Her parents hired me. For various reasons we thought she might have decided to spend time here."

The woman shook her head. "We don't have anyone here by that name. She's an actress?"

"Yes. She's only twenty-four but was nominated for an Academy Award."

"My word. I don't know who's who in Hollywood anymore. But Robert Redford is my favorite. I also liked Paul Newman, too, may he rest in peace."

"Maybe Cleo registered under a different name," Regan said hurriedly. "She drives a white SUV with California plates. We saw one outside. Who does that belong to?"

"Oh, I think that car belongs to Connie Long."

"Connie Long?" Regan asked.

"Yes. She's here writing a book. Let me go back and check the files."

77

C leo placed her empty wineglass on the coffee table. "Time to go." She turned to Dirk. "But before I leave I want to tell you something."

"What's that?" he asked, touching her arm softly.

"I'm an actress."

"Really? I can tell you're talented. I'll bet you'll get a break one of these days. You'd better finish that book, though."

Cleo laughed. "Actually, I'm not writing a book. And I've already had my break. I was even nominated for an Academy Award this year but lost. Have you ever heard of the movie *My Super Super?*"

A dumbfounded Dirk shook his head. "I didn't see the movie but my sister and my mother did. They both loved it and kept talking about the crazy super . . ." He paused. "Wait a minute. Are you Cleo Paradise?"

Cleo nodded. "I wanted to tell you before we spent any more time together because I don't want you to think I was playing games. In a few days I'll be meeting up with my best friend, Daisy, and we'll drive back to California together. She's working on a movie in Florida now."

"Oh." Dirk was quiet for a moment, then continued, "I hope that doesn't mean I'll never see you again."

"Of course not."

"I liked you from the minute I saw you. It doesn't matter to me whether you're Connie Long or Cleo Paradise."

"I realize that," Cleo said. "To some people it would make a difference." She paused. "They would never ever get involved with an actress!"

Dirk grinned, then leaned over and kissed her. He drew back his head, looked into her eyes, and gently pushed her hair from her forehead. "You won't get mad at me, then, if I call you Connie by accident? Because to me, you'll always be Connie."

Cleo smiled. "Call me Connie all the time."

They kissed again.

"Until tomorrow." Cleo stood. "You'll be all right hobbling around on that foot tonight?"

"I'll be fine. I wish I could walk you to your cabin. Take the flashlight by the door. Call me when you get inside."

"I will," Cleo said, not wanting to admit she was nervous about walking to the cabin alone.

"Thanks, Connie."

Cleo laughed and leaned down for one more kiss.

The stranger outside the window seethed. Why not me, Cleo? Why not me?

78

Yes, that white SUV does belong to Connie Long."

"Did you see Connie?" Regan asked.

"Just from the window. She was going swimming with the owner of the camp."

"How old is she?"

"In her early twenties. Petite, light brown hair. Adorable."

"That sounds like Cleo. Maybe she registered under the name Connie Long. Can we call her cabin?" Regan asked.

"There are no phones in the cabins. Miss Long was with the owner today. Let me call his cell phone."

"Fine," Regan answered. She and Jack waited while the woman picked up the phone and dialed.

"Dirk?"

"Yes, Mrs. Briggs."

"There's a private investigator here looking for an actress named Cleo Paradise. She showed me her credentials and seems to think that Miss Long might be Cleo."

"Can I speak to the investigator?"

"Certainly." Mrs. Briggs handed Regan the phone.

"Hello, this is Regan Reilly."

"Hello, Regan. My name is Dirk Tapper. You're looking for Cleo Paradise?"

"Yes. Her parents are terribly worried because they haven't been able to reach her. So is her best friend."

"They don't have to worry. She just left my cabin. She's been here for hours." He laughed. "We were having a good time."

"Oh, that's wonderful!" Regan exclaimed. "I can't wait to have Cleo call them. They'll be so relieved. Can you tell me where her cabin is? I'd like to talk to her in person for a few minutes."

"She's in Cabin Number Four. Mrs. Briggs can point out which trail you should take. Cleo's cabin isn't far from the office. I'd take you up there myself but I sprained my ankle. Please grab one of the little flashlights on the counter there. Let me speak to Mrs. Briggs, please."

"Thanks so much. I really appreciate it." Regan handed the phone back to Mrs. Briggs.

"Connie Long is really a famous actress named Cleo Paradise? My goodness," Mrs. Briggs said to Dirk. "Yes, I'll show them!" A moment later she walked around the counter, led Regan and Jack out the door, and pointed to the right. "See that trail in the middle? Connie or Cleo or whatever her name is, is in the first cabin at the top of the hill. You've got your flashlight but there are also red reflectors on either side of the trail to guide you."

"Thanks again," Regan said.

"You're welcome."

Outside Dirk's cabin, Cleo's old fears surfaced. Her heart was pounding as she hurried down the steep path, shining the flashlight in front of her. Images of her bathing suit on the clothesline flashed through her mind. She started to move faster. It will be OK, she told herself. I'll be in my cabin in a few minutes and I'll call Dirk and then Daisy. I can't wait to tell her about my day with him. The sound of a twig snapping in the woods terrified her. Did that sound come from behind me? Cleo broke into a sweat and started to run, not stopping until she reached the front door of her cabin.

Jack had the flashlight in his hand. He and Regan crossed the parking lot and started up the trail.

"The owner sounded really nice," Regan reported. "He said Cleo had been in his cabin since early afternoon. What a relief!"

"Sometimes there's a simple explanation for these things," Jack said.

In the distance they could see a woman standing in front of Cleo's cabin, flashlight in hand. She pushed open the door, flicked on the outside light, then started inside.

A figure wearing a ski mask emerged from the darkness, knife in one hand, flowers in the other, and rushed to push his way into Cleo's cabin.

"Oh my God!" Regan cried as she and Jack took off up the trail.

Cleo screamed as she struggled to close the door. She was pushing as hard as she could, but was finally thrown backward. "No!" she screamed as she landed on the floor. "No!"

The intruder rushed into the cabin and threw a bouquet at Cleo. She tried to get away, but he caught her arm. "You'll never say no to me again, Cleo! Never!" He raised the knife.

Jack Reilly lunged forward and grabbed the man's wrists

firmly from behind. "Oh, I think she will," Jack shouted, tightening his grip.

Cleo scurried backward as the knife fell to the floor.

The intruder howled in pain. Regan yanked off his ski mask.

It was Winston.

79

———◆———

Why doesn't anyone like me?" Winston screamed as he was being led off in handcuffs. "All I do is try and help people."

Regan's cell phone rang. She cringed when she realized it was Kit calling. I'll never hear the end of this, she thought.

"Hey, Kit."

"Regan, are you busy?"

"Kind of."

"I'll make this quick," Kit said. "I was about to pick up the phone to call Winston a few minutes ago. I'd been debating since this afternoon when I bought a women's magazine with a headline that said you're too picky if you're not married. You know, basically you're a picky loser."

"Right."

"But then I remembered something that struck me as weird. Winston said he came from a large family. I was so bored on our date that my mind was drifting in and out in an effort to protect my sanity. He was completely obsessed by the invertebrates . . ."

"Uh-huh."

"Regan, I'm almost positive he said he didn't have a sister. I think he was lying to you, for some reason. So I decided not to call him."

"Good move, Kit. He would have been too busy to talk."

"What do you mean?"

"Kit, Jack and I found Cleo."

"That's great! Where?"

"At a log cabin camp in New Jersey. Winston was here, too. We arrived in the nick of time. Winston was about to stab her."

"What? Oh my God, Regan! Is Cleo okay?"

"She's shaken up, but she's fine. We reached Cleo's parents and her best friend who are out of their minds with relief. They'll all be in New Jersey tomorrow. Turned out Winston tried to come to Cleo's aid when she got knocked over by a wave on the beach when she first got to Edna's. He offered to walk her home but she refused. It seems his obsession turned from invertebrates to Cleo. We don't know much more yet."

Kit hurled the magazine across her living room. "Reilly, the people you set me up with!"

"I know, Kit. Why don't you come down to the Shore this weekend? It's my mother's birthday Saturday. Something tells me we'll be having a big celebration."

Saturday, August 6th

80

In the Reillys' backyard in Spring Lake, Jack and Luke were slaving over a sizzling grill, every square inch filled with steaks, chicken, hot dogs, and hamburgers.

"Whatever happened to dinner for four at a quiet restaurant?" Luke muttered, his blue eyes twinkling with amusement.

Jack laughed. "You know Nora likes any excuse for a big party."

Regan and Nora came from the kitchen carrying trays stacked with hot dog and hamburger rolls.

"What are you two laughing about?" Nora asked.

Luke put his arm around his wife, then kissed the top of her head. "We were talking about how relaxing it is to barbecue."

"Oh, you, I couldn't think of a better way to celebrate my birthday."

"I'm just kidding," Luke said. "This is wonderful."

"Dad, tomorrow Jack and I will take you and Mom to brunch at the Breakers. You can relax and be waited on."

Luke's eyes twinkled. "Party of twelve?"

Regan shook her head. "I think you're just jealous you missed all the excitement."

"I am. While you were solving crimes, I was stuck in bumper-to-bumper traffic on the Garden State Parkway."

Jack winked at Regan. She glanced around at the crowd. "Everyone is having a great time."

Cleo and Dirk were standing with their arms around each other.

"You know, Cleo," Dirk's mother said for the twelfth time, "when I spoke to you on the phone the other day, your voice sounded so familiar. I should have guessed it was you. I could kick myself. I saw *My Super Super* three times! You deserved to win the Academy Award. They stole it from you, they really did!"

Cleo smiled. "Thank you."

"What movie are you doing next?"

"I don't know. I'm waiting until the contract with my current agent runs out next week. Then I'll see what I'm offered."

Daisy groaned. "Good riddance!" She turned to Dizzy. "Whatever you do, don't sign with the Flake Agency!"

"I won't," Dizzy promised as Monique looked at him adoringly. Their kids were running around the yard, croquet mallets in hand, whacking the colorful, heavy balls with great vigor. Judson was trying to teach them how to play. The video of Dizzy putting up the beach umbrella had gone viral overnight. He was now entertaining several movie offers. "But whoever I end up with, I'm going to tell them I'll only do comedy. No more drama!"

"You said it," Monique agreed, smiling. "Cleo, you're sure that guy on the motorcycle who left the flowers is harmless?"

Cleo nodded. "Daisy made some calls and found out it's most likely a guy from our old acting class who drives a Harley-Davidson. He can't get arrested in Hollywood, so he started pulling those kinds of harmless pranks hoping to get attention. I never reported it, which must have really frustrated him."

"Good," Monique said. "That kind of prank isn't funny."

"Thanks to Tommy, we were able to figure it out," Cleo said.

"Show business is so competitive," Daisy said. "I wouldn't have been surprised if April Dockton had been the one after Cleo. I heard she retreated to a yoga camp in Lenox, Massachusetts, after hearing from another producer that he wanted Cleo for his movie, not her. I can testify to the fact that she really needs that yoga," Daisy joked, massaging her throat. "I thought she was really going to kill me when I worked with her. All because I'm Cleo's friend."

"Dirk," Yaya said breezily, deliberately changing the subject. "Cliff and I just love your log cabins. Yours is the best camp we've ever been to. And as you know, we've been all over the world."

Dirk smiled. "I hope you'll visit often."

"We will," Cliff stated vehemently. "On Monday we start scouting locations for our museum. It will definitely be somewhere in New Jersey. Mrs. Briggs and Gordy have graciously offered to help us."

"Absolutely," Mrs. Briggs nodded.

Edna and Wilbur were sitting at a table with Karen, Frankie, and Rhonda, and several of their cronies from Golden Peaks.

"If I never had the garage sale," Edna said, "I wouldn't have met Regan. Which means she and Jack would never have saved Cleo. Despite those miserable cheats, my garage sale couldn't have turned out better."

"Mom," Karen said, "give me some credit, too. I'm the one who sent Nora over to your sale in the first place."

"Whatever," Edna shrugged, then picked up her glass. "Rhonda, welcome to the family."

"Thank you." Rhonda turned to Frankie who gave her a quick kiss.

"That's so nice," Edna said. "You know, Frankie, I could still try and see if my buyer would agree to cancel the deal on the house."

"No thanks, Mom. We're fine," Frankie said quickly. He lifted his glass. "Wilbur, it's a pleasure to also welcome you to the family."

Wilbur and Edna had gotten engaged. She'd sealed the deal in the emergency room.

Hayley and Kit were becoming fast friends, comparing war stories about their love lives.

"I still can't believe that guy Scott," Hayley said. "He's nothing but a lying crook. With a fake charity no less! Can you believe he pretended to get engaged to win people's trust so he could scam them? And then he used pictures taken of himself with celebrities at the events I brought him to? What a sleaze!"

"At least he didn't try to kill anyone," Kit muttered. "Can you believe that when the cops went to Winston's apartment they found pictures of Cleo on every wall and copies of her movies with a receipt from July 8th, when he bought them? That's the day after he tried to help her on the beach. He certainly got over me fast. And his mother asked the police to have sympathy for him because the only girlfriend he ever had jilted him at the altar!"

"I don't think anyone's going to ask for sympathy for Scott," Hayley said. She raised her glass, "Here's to the next one."

After dinner, Regan and Jack carried out Nora's birthday cake, which was a sheet of flames.

"Regan, half a dozen candles would have been plenty," Nora protested as the crowd started to sing "Happy Birthday."

"You haven't seen anything yet," Regan said, raising an eye-brow.

At nine o'clock Cliff Paradise called for everyone's attention. "My wife Yaya and I are thrilled to be with you all tonight," he said. "We are so grateful for Cleo's safety. Many of you had a part in her rescue, especially, of course, Regan and Jack Reilly. We can never thank you enough.

"Before this, I wasn't familiar with New Jersey. Now it will always be a special place for my family. We've met so many wonderful people here. Would everyone please come around to the front of the house so we can look out over the ocean and celebrate our new friendships?"

They all followed him.

A moment later the sky was ablaze with fireworks, enjoyed by thousands along the Jersey Shore.

Regan rested her head on Jack's shoulder. "What do you want to do next weekend?"

"Come back here."

Regan nodded. "Me, too."